CW00386131

*Imagination is the grea
all*

Always believe in yourself

*Thank you to Rosemary and Lois
for being the best proof readers an
author could wish for*

*Sam, for all your hours spend editing
my books*

TO LYNNE
ALways believe
in yourself.

Author's Words

I would like to take this time to thank you all for believing in me and joining me and Joe on this magical journey. Throughout the worldwide pandemic I never thought that this would be more than a few words on a page but look where we are now, two books with more potentially on the way. Thank you for all the love and support that you all have shown me throughout. The belief you have bestowed on me has been an authors dream. For a person who suffers from dyslexia, writing a book comes with many personal challenges and its your support that has helped me overcome these challenges and many more. Thank you from the bottom of my heart and I really hope you enjoy part two of this ever changing magical world. The illustrations in this book have been created by some of the students from Marpool Primary School who worked with me during one of my author visits, this visit was incredibly special for me as this was the school were many of the characters from the book first came to life in my imagination.

Uncle Barry

Lady Malaga

Lady Malaga

Contents

Chapter 1

WORLD'S APART

Can you all remember when I was cast in that dark and dingy cell and I was amazed to find the magnificent rainbow tree, this was the world I was truly waiting for but I'm getting ahead of myself. I first ended up in headquarters and I met some people I will call friends for life, along with some mysterious teachers. Remember when I had to save Patrick from taking the blame for showing me the forbidden magic, they say everything happens for a reason. Patrick sacrificed a lot to protect me from that cell and of course Lady Malaga. His spell transported me to another world where I could live and finish my training to become the warlock I was born to become. Patrick truly is one of my greatest friends and I knew the time would come when I would get the chance to repay the favour and save the entire human race. The plan was for me to scarper from headquarters, taking the old forbidden magic book with me. Blue was another one of my greatest friends and had made Patrick promise to look out for me as he could foresee me being cast out.

They came up with the idea of the book and knew that it would break so many of the dreaded rules we had to follow. The magic contained inside this book was old magic that could end up causing havoc if it ever got into the wrong hands. It was Blue's idea to use this as bait and he ultimately knew I would be the one to help them all, I knew I had to be ready for what was about to unfold. The world I ended up in was the same place that everyone who was cast out was sent to, the ends of the earth. Once you were sent there you could never escape, but Blue knew I would be the one that could end this, they all knew Lady Malaga wanted me for something and knew she would come after me but only when I was a fully trained warlock. I knew that I would be the key to her final spell.

Ten years had passed since I had been cast in to this world and I had managed to keep in touch with my family through dreams and letters but it had been three hundred and sixty five days since I had last heard anything. You could say that I was the strongest warlock I could be and was so proud of all the obstacles I had overcome. Every day I hoped and prayed that the outside world was still alright since I had no way of knowing. Do you all remember the time when Lara and Lady Malaga had spent all of that time planning something together? Well I found out that Lara had been frozen and would be released when the time was right. Blue mentioned that the Dark Gardens was where Lady Malaga was building her army, once she had trained and manipulated them to become the best they could be, she would force them to enter a frozen stasis until she was ready for her master plan to become reality. I knew the time had come when she would be coming for me and she would stop at nothing to cross the border of this world. She knew that I was at my strongest and she would burn this world to ashes to get her hands on me again. I needed to get away from this place to make sure all the inhabitants of this world could be safe, I would find a way back eventually and free them all from their heartache in this everlasting prison. I strongly doubted that Lady Malaga had a heart because during my ten year stint in this world, hundreds if not thousands of warlocks had been cast here without hurting or killing them. I had a glimmer of hope that she still had a little warmth encased in the shell of her heart. Just two days separated me from leaving this place but I still had so much to learn if I wanted to make sure that no harm came to this world. Many of the warlocks that had been cast here had tried to escape but had found themselves turned to ash. Lady Malaga would never kill but if you decided to leave then it was your choice to die and not hers, I believe her mother must have taught her this dark magic.

My time in the ends of the earth had been great and I had learnt so much about myself but I did miss the headquarters weirdly though. Lara, Patrick and Blue were always on my mind, not to mention some of the teachers that I had come across during my time there. During my walks around this place, the rainbow tree was still standing and just as colourful and bright as it was ten years ago. I couldn't believe that I was now twenty five years old. I left home when I was just fifteen, I knew this was going to be a very strange chapter of my life as I had to make some big decisions. I couldn't wait to go back home and see everyone again including my magical twin, I often wondered if the spell had truly worked and that Joe was still with us and that everyone's memories had been updated to believe that he had always been with us and not created by magic.

What if my Mum and Dad had trained up Joe to become a warlock as well, I couldn't wait to see everyone and find out. I knew I had to first prepare myself to get the leaving spell just right at precisely the right time, midnight if you were wondering. The people here had become like another family to me, a home away from home, most of the warlocks that had been cast here had lost the use of their magic and some had managed to retain some. Blue on the other hand had somehow managed to keep all of his, so he had once again become my trainer and the best one at that. Ned was also here with me but time had not been kind to him and the magic that once pulsed throughout him had started to diminish and was not going to last much longer. I needed to help him and his sister who was still trapped in the dark gardens back at headquarters. Blue had helped me become the man I am today, the last spell that I had learnt completed my warlock ring and Blue had cried a little. I had also been helping Blue with the training of the other warlocks sent here when they hadn't met Lady Malaga's grade every couple of months, only those that had managed to keep their magic though. The others would help everyone by collecting wood to keep the fires burning or making sure we all had substantial meals by catching fish, it was a lot better than headquarters.

Throughout the years I had been training everyday, working to get more stones placed within my ring. I was so lucky that Blue had managed to keep his magic, he was so powerful that nothing could really hurt him. I didn't know how old he was but with his knowledge of magic, I knew he had been around for a long time and was one of the most powerful warlocks I have ever met. I remembered when we had been reunited ten years ago, when he was running towards me, I could not believe my eyes. I thought I had lost him forever when Lady Malaga had cast him into this world. He had shown me around this land, it was so colourful that the brightness almost hurt your eyes which was a shock as this was called the ends of the earth. Blue explained that this used to be black and grey with no colour or love. Luckily for us Lady Malaga cast a warlock here and she was very colourful, the moment she arrived here, the other warlocks could not believe their eyes, everything went from dark and void of life to bright and colourful just like a rainbow within minutes. From the leaves on the trees down to the insects roaming the ground. The warlock was called Mrs Colour and everything she touched would change to all the colours of the rainbow, this now explained the rainbow I had first seen when I was cast here. Blue got teary eyes as he explained that Mrs Colour had sacrificed herself for the good of everyone else here, she had tried to cast an exit spell and this had not worked and Mrs Colour had been banished to ash like everyone else who had tried to escape. Luckily for all of us left here, Mrs Colour has left her love and colour in this land and everything has been stained her unique rainbow colours.

We all got together every year on the eighth of November to gather around the rainbow tree. This is where we would all cast up a message to hang on the tree in Mrs Colour's memory, some of the people here also said that she was the only one to stand up to Lady Malaga and even got a strike at her, but she wasn't strong enough. Lady Malaga had tried to cast a spell over Mrs Colour to trap her in a spell book for all eternity but Mrs Colour was too powerful for the spell to take a hold of her. Lady

Malaga was left with one option and that was to cast her to the ends of the earth. There were whispers that Lady Malaga had heard of the magic Mrs Colour had cast over this land and had tried to put a stop to it, but Mrs Colour had a trick up her sleeve and had managed to keep the dreaded witch out.

When word reached Lady Malaga of Mrs Colour's escape attempt, a huge party was thrown at headquarters with everything decorated in ash to resemble what Mrs Colour had become. The other warlocks at headquarters were so sad as they were not allowed to show any emotion as the punishments that would follow would be too harsh.

Ten years had passed since I was cast to this land and every day was the same, being trained by Blue. Some days I would not eat as I knew I wanted to become the best warlock I had been training to be. I would stay up most nights reading every spell book I could get my hands on. Blue had all the spells trapped inside his head but had kindly created many books for all those who had managed to keep their magic. Everyday he would remind us that there was a war coming and that this would affect the warlock world along with the human race.

Warlocks are more powerful than humans, all warlocks were born human but that all changed when they got their rings woken by the deep magic. When this happened the human part of our souls died and the warlock part was empowered. A prophecy was always told that there was one warlock that would change everything and this was of course, me. I knew of the impending war and that I was going to be the one to stop it, I would never let Lady Malaga control the spell that could control all warlocks and capture the human race and turn them into her slaves.

I remembered the time when I was at Uncle Barry's and I ventured into the past and saw the little old man who worked out how to control the same spell that she was after. I couldn't remember it at the time but those memories have returned to me and I do now. I was too afraid to speak the spell in case Lady Malaga heard it through her magic, she knows that I remember it and will stop at nothing to get her hands on it. I can remember the day when I had finished my last training test and looked down at my ring, to my astonishment I saw the the last stone fit into my ring. A burst of light erupted from my ring which encased my whole body. All of the spells I had ever learnt flashed before my very own eyes and then the memories of the past flitted through my mind. Blue had witnessed my transformation from a young boy into a man, everyone here looks up to me like a brother as we are a very close knit family.

Before Mrs Colour had made the ultimate sacrifice, she made sure she had left her life force and love which had bestowed on the land, numerous orchards filled with all manner of fruit and lakes full of fresh fish. At times Blue would allow us to conjure up bread to go with all of the things Mrs Colour had left us, this was not always the case because Blue needed to make sure conflict would not erupt between those who had managed to keep their magic and those who had lost their gift. There was one warlock who thought he was highly amusing by deciding to go down the dreaded route of evil magic, his name was Dev. Blue had seen a big change in Dev when he tried to open up a portal for Lady Malaga to roam this world. When he was a student at headquarters he constantly went against her rules and this left her no choice but to banish him here, a lot of the other warlocks could not understand why he had tried to make her come back to this place. Ever since he had come here he would try and contact Lady Malaga to utter his apologies but these fell on deaf ears, each time he attempted to do this, Lady Malaga would cast a dark spell on his body leaving him with dark scars that cut deeply across his back. When Blue found out he had been talking to her, he took matters into his own hands and cast a sleeping spell on Dev, once he was asleep Blue trapped him into a bubble of smoke and plunged him into the bottom of the lake. Whispers had started to echo across the land that Dev would awaken and continue on his mission to open this portal for Lady Malaga's dreaded return. When this news had reached Blue he had stationed those who had kept their magic at the edge of the lake to keep an eye on Dev, we all had to be ready in case Blue's spell was broken.

We all lived in a long hut that we all added to as time went on, it was the best we could muster with what we had to work with. We would find old logs and twigs to build onto the old hut, it wasn't great but it was home. We all pulled together on a daily basis to get the jobs done that needed to be done, Blue would never let the standards that Mrs Colour had set, slip. No one wanted to carry on after her death especially those who were tasked with the upkeep of our home, it took an enormous amount of effort from Blue to keep everyone's spirits up, even Dev took her death hard which some say is what turned him rotten.

Every day there was always some sort of drama going on, some didn't want to work hard for their spells and some had just lost their way. Blue had created a magical space on the opposite side of the lake where you could go and take a time out if you ever felt like you had had enough. The space was filled with trees with hammocks hanging from the branches for you to relax on and even a swing roped from the high branches. You could lie and watch the world go by for hours watching the ripples of the lake and the occasional jump of the fish from the depths below. You could take food to this place if you wanted but the maximum time you could spend here would be two days. Only one warlock was allowed into this place at once and Blue's rules dictated that if you were on a time out you had to be by yourself and recharge. Blue's rules were very strict and for very good reason, we could never lose hope and the warlocks could never fall.

Day after day I would train other students up to help Blue out, it only seemed like yesterday that I was casting my first spell. Blue reckoned I could be as strong as Lady Malaga and that I should never lose faith in myself and start to believe that everything I had trained for was possible. It was starting to become tougher each day when I didn't receive word from home in the form of letters or dreams and I became more frustrated as time went on. I knew that one day I would love to have my own training school for warlocks where everyone would be respected and trained to be the best they could be. The next few days would be a mad rush as we had so much to accomplish to make sure we protected everyone, humans and warlocks alike. I wonder if Lady Malaga has changed at all, does she look much different or even act any different than she did when we first met. I haven't even heard anything from her but my gut feeling tells me that I will be facing her very soon.

Suddenly there was a shout from the edge of the lake. A warlock called Tommy that was on guard duty shouted 'The water is moving, it is moving.'

Everyone dashed out of the hut to see what the commotion was and looked towards the lake. The water had started to rush much faster than normal and we all ran towards it. The low water in the lake started to climb higher up the banks of the shore. Suddenly the water shot apart into two columns twenty foot high. Everyone started to dash back towards the hut as some of the warlocks had been drenched with the force of the water.

Blue shouted out 'Get back, my spell is coming to an end that was keeping Dev safe. He will soon wake up and my spell will be weak enough for him to break free, we all have to be ready.'

Everyone gathered around in a circle ready to cast a spell to hold Dev longer, we had all been standing like this for twenty minutes anxiously waiting for something to happen. The water was still being held up by some invisible force, suddenly it crashed back into the lake causing a tsunami effect. I cast a magic cloud of smoke to protect everyone, which enveloped us all and raised us up off the ground. The wave was crashing towards our hut to destroy our months of hard work, Blue broke out of our circle and flew towards the wave and with a casual flick of his ring the wave began its retreat back towards the lake. Everyone started to cheer and clap Blue and his awesome ability to wield magic, he joined us back in the circle and told us that we all had to cast the gravity spell as this would hold Dev in his temporary prison for a few more hours so we could prepare for his return. No matter what we tried there was nothing we could do to hold him down any longer, we all cast out which felt like an eternity. Some of us were forced against the shore and the water and escaped with minor scrapes and bruises. We held him there for another two hours, Blue watched the magical clock he had conjured into existence making sure we were doing everything we could. None of us knew what Dev would be like when he finally woke up from his deep slumber, one thing I knew for sure was that I would not let any harm come to those I considered family.

It was getting late and the sunset was ebbing towards the horizon and darkness would soon settle over this land. We all knew this was the time we would face Dev once and for all. One of the warlocks ran inside the hut to fetch lanterns, these would be filled with warlock light that would burn bright for the whole night. Sophie was the warlock who managed to run out with six lanterns. Everyone wondered why Sophie was cast to the ends of the earth, some say this was because she was so beautiful Lady Malaga had got jealous. Sophie was always top of the class and got the best grades in her training but she was told she would be no good for the army because she did not pull her weight. She conjured up her warlock light and the six lanterns floated into the sky above the lake. Blue shouted 'Well done you are well on your way to becoming a great warlock.'

Sophie did not know how to take the praise and redness started to creep into her cheeks, she hated any form of praise in front of other warlocks. Sophie only had around another month to go before she earns the final stone in her ring and her warlock training would become complete. It would be a shame as I would not get to see her graduate, I had made a promise to Sophie that I would come back to save everyone, we had become close friends over the years. Sophie has been banished here five years after me, she hated Lady Malaga and wanted revenge on her for everything she had done to her and her family.

Lady Malaga thinks she is all might and powerful going out and hunting people who she thinks will be great for her army. She doesn't even care if it rips the family apart taking away the children and sometimes even the parents. Lady Malaga had been doing this for years now but for the past few years had been keeping a low profile until her army was complete. We all knew Lady Malaga was waiting to exact revenge for her mother's death.

A terrifying smashing sound hit the air caused by the lanterns blowing up one by one, Blue knew something was up and he was busy getting everyone ready for Dev's return. From deep within the lake a light from dark blue to black, the water that was once still appeared to crack open and split into two this time going deeper into the lake instead of the air, the split got wider and wider. A beam of light shot out of the depths of the lake quicker than you could blink, a fifty foot drop had appeared in the centre of the lake. Out of the fifty foot drop flew Dev, faster than humanly possible, I looked over to Blue and could see the concern etched on his face. I knew I would never let anything happen to Blue and closed my fingers in a tight grip ready to face off with Dev.

Blue knew he had to do something and cast out to lift himself from the ground, once he was flying through the air, Blue cast out again this time to make him go turbo. Dev looked on with an amused look upon his face and charged head on towards Blue. They both cast a spell towards each other which collided mere metres in front of the casters. The spells were so powerful it caused the ground to start to tremble which felt like the rumbling of an earthquake. I looked up into the air and as the spell residue started to die away I could not see either Blue or Dev. This could not be happening, Blue could not be gone again.

The sky was covered in a smoke that blocked out most natural vision. I called out for Blue but there was no sign of him. I shouted out again as the smoke started to clear and suddenly there he was, floating towards the ground like a cloud with no signs of life. I cast out and flew up to catch Blue, I caught him and safely brought Blue to the ground. As we landed I looked into the sky and noticed a huge tear in the very fabric of the sky like someone had torn a hole right through it. Blue started to come around and I could tell he was in shock, the pure strength of the spell had taken its toll on him. Blue pointed towards the sky and said 'He's completed the spell, the portal has been opened, she will soon be here. You are our only hope Joe, promise me that you will stop her.'

Blue's eyes flitted closed and I knew that he had to rest. I conjured up a stretcher that would allow me to get Blue to the safety of our hut. I called all of the other warlocks into the safety of our home and sealed the doors closed with a magic only the purest of heart could attempt. This would keep us safe for now, I warned all of the other warlocks that the portal had been opened and we were all at risk and to get ready for the upcoming return of Lady Malaga.

Chapter 2

THE PORTAL

All of the warlocks were getting ready for the return of Lady Malaga, none of them seemed scared at all that she could just turn up out of the blue. Everyone started to gather outside of the hut to try and come up with a plan, we all knew that we had to be brave and stick together to show that we were united against the evil that was Lady Malaga. We would not let anything happen to the community that we had built up over the past ten years.

I knew that to stop her coming I would have to return to her, I didn't want to tell anyone else as I knew they all would want to help me but none of them were able to stand up against her might.

We stood outside of the hut looking up at the sky for what felt like hours, the portal looked as if it was getting bigger by the minute. Suddenly a crash from inside the hut startled us all, I dashed inside the hut and found Blue was up and walking about, looking for the things he needed to make himself a hot drink. He walked outside to check if anyone else wanted a hot drink, as soon as he entered the hut again, several bolts of lightning flashed its way out of the inside of the portal. The lightning left gaping holes that still smoked with the after effects, we all ran to the safety of our hut. We looked out of the windows and saw that another bolt of lightning struck the depths of the lake, lighting it up with the oddest shades of green and yellow.

We heard Blue shout for us to get down and get to cover, we all ducked down to hide from the brewing storm outside. Blue slammed the door and sealed it shut with the force of his magic. Sophie turned to Blue and said 'What is all this fuss about, it's only a few bolts of lightning.'

Blue looked at Sophie with horror etched onto his face and replied 'Not just any lightning Sophie, take a look for yourself.'

Sophie looked out of the window and saw that the lightning that kept striking the ground was filled with evil magic that had caused sharp spikes to hit everything they came into contact with. One had forced its way into the side of our hut cutting through the wall like it was butter.

Blue told us to cast out a spell for protection, we cast out a force field that surrounded the hut. Luckily the spell was cast just in time as a rogue spike smashed a large hole through the door. Multiple spikes smashed into the force field, which bounced away with the force of the magic we had all poured into our spell. We all knew this was the doing of Lady Malaga, Blue confirmed this to us all as he had seen this type of magic before. We still didn't know when she would arrive and I could sense that everyone was apprehensive.

One of the warlocks who was called Henry, thought he was clever and decided to run through the force field as he was not scared of the dreaded Lady Malaga. Sophie tried to stop him but he was too quick as he dashed through the hole that the spikes had previously made. Once he was outside we all turned to Blue and begged for him to release the protective force field but he told us that it was too late. We watched as the lightning snapped through the sky and hit Henry's feet. It lifted him up forcing him towards the portal, we knew there was nothing we could do to help him anymore. Henry's face and body started to morph as the bolts of lightning changed to an eerily black colour.

Blue shouted out to us 'There you go, she's here'

We all continued to look at what was unfolding outside of the window, it was completely devastating to see Henry fading away minute by minute and suddenly she was there in all of her evilness, Lady Malaga.

She looked over at the hut and burst out laughing her evil yet enchanting laugh 'So this is where all the fun is, shame about all of this colour… This will never do, let us change that back' She erupted into her laugh once again and began to cast, black smoke spun its way from her fingers that covered our once beautiful land. As the smoke hit everything in its path, the colour that had been magicked into existence by Mrs Colour, disappeared. In its place stood a dark, dark world void of any life.

Lady Malaga floated down from her perch high on one of the lightning bolts and threw Henry's body down towards the lake like it was an old rag doll.

She shouted out to us 'Now I think you all know why I am here, I want the boy… Yet you're not a boy anymore are you Joe?

She continued with her laughter and a flash of light erupted from her fingers and hit our hut, blasting it to pieces in front of our very eyes. Slivers of our magic force field dropped before our eyes and we knew our spell had been broken. Lady Malaga flew towards us and her red eyes were the only colour left in our void of a world. This was now truly the prison she had intended this place to be.

She looked me squarely in the eyes and spoke out clearly 'There you are Joe, it has been a long time, haven't you grown. You have what I want, give it up or watch your little friends suffer before you.'

She then vanished leaving behind a trace of her evil magic.

I knew I couldn't let her hurt anyone and she had to be stopped. The bolt of lightning stopped the relentless pounding of the earth and disappeared. The portal kept growing and turned a vibrant shade of red. Blue told us that it wouldn't be long until her cursed fire torched this land and destroyed it forever and I knew that this could never happen.

Blue and I knew that this was my time to face her and that I needed to get out of this place. How I was going to achieve this was a different story, things could be sent to this world but could not leave. What had happened to Mrs Colour had devastated all those around me and I had to practise to make sure I got this right.

Everyone was solemn with the events that Lady Malaga had just caused and no one knew what to do with themselves. Some sat crying whilst others walked around looking downtrodden and disheartened. Our home had been destroyed by an evil no one ever thought possible, Blue said that he wanted to rebuild our structure of hope and love but to do so we would all need to pull together and not let evil into our hearts. We didn't know if it was even possible to overcome the damage caused by Lady Malaga as we didn't know the extent of her evil magic and if this could be erased by the pure magic that we carried within us. Our once lush green world that was filled with so much colour was now a cold and empty miserable place. Blue cast a spell towards the remaining shards of our hut to try and restore it to its former glory. Each time he tried the hut crumbled under the weight of the pure evil residue left behind. With every attempt I could sense Blue's magic wavering. Was there any hope left for the rest of the warlocks or would everyday now be a fight for survival.

I remembered what I was told of the legacy of Mrs Colour and how she had cast this land full of love and happiness. I looked over to the rainbow tree and nearly wept at the sight before my eyes. Gone was the once bright cheerful tree and in its place stood a tree buckling under the sheer evilness left behind. I noticed a glint from behind the tree and made a run for it, I reached the tree just in time and one of the branch's snapped and floated towards the ground. I thought I could hear Mrs Colour's voice on the wind, urging me to save her legacy. Blue shouted over to me 'That's the tree of love and hope Joe, bring me that branch, this could be the saving grace that we need.'

The branch started to rise up towards the portal and I made a jump for it, as I did it floated higher and higher away from me. I sensed this was a test from none other than Mrs Colour herself. I cast out a spell to fly towards the branch and began my chase towards it, it climbed so high it was almost to the portal. As I neared the portal, I could feel its magic pushing me back towards the ground, Sophie could see that I was struggling to catch the glowing branch, she flew up towards me and attempted to help me catch the branch. As Sophie climbed to the same altitude that I was, the magic of the portal threw Sophie like she weighed nothing more than a feather. It threw her several feet back towards the now ever dead trees on the ground, she was thrown so fast she nearly passed out with the force of the magic ensnaring her body. I flew towards Sophie to save her from hitting anything and hurting herself.

Blue shouted up to us 'This is a test to see if you have what it takes to save us with your love and courage, you can both do it and must not give in.'

All of the warlocks started to cast out and were flying into the air, we all knew that we needed to work as a team. The branch seemed to have its own mind and it started its dive back towards the ground then suddenly changed its course and flew back into the air narrowly missing the other warlocks. Blue staying solidly back on the ground as he knew this was our test and not one he could get involved in. We knew this was about loving each other and working together to save us from evil. Everyone focussed on the branch and dashed through the air trying to catch it, with each passing minute the colour was fading. This was our only chance to restore this land to what it once was.

Blue shouted again 'Come on all of you, I truly believe in you all but you only have one chance at this.'

Blue's words spurred everyone on and you could sense the change of mindset. One warlock almost caught it but didn't quite succeed. Sophie looked towards me and mouthed that the branch was getting smaller. This test was one of the hardest we as a team had to endure, the failing light in the sky was making the branch nearly impossible to see. I suddenly remembered one of my previous tests where I was told to use my mind to create the sense of feeling, I calmed my mind and began to see the branch in my mind's eye, I reached out my hand and to my astonishment I caught the branch. Suddenly the branch began to grow in size doubling its weight. It became so heavy it was a test in itself to keep a hold of it, I could feel it pulling me towards the ground. I plummeted towards the ground and heard the whispers of magic all around me. The warlocks on the ground had begun to cast out to break my fall.

The branch stuck itself into the ground and the colour ebbed its way from the very centre of the branch into the earth. Everything became so bright it was almost impossible to keep our eyes open. A shadow appeared to one side of the branch and whispered to us all 'My warlocks, you have shown me that you have love and courage in all of your hearts, this is my last gift to you all. Enjoy this magic as this cannot be harmed by the evil that has possessed this land for too long.'

The shadow that was Mrs Colour melted away and was sucked back into the branch, all that was left behind was a rainbow coloured rock, which was etched with the words, throw me to the depths of the lake.

I picked up the rock and walked to the edge of the lake, you could still feel the evilness that had been left behind from Lady Malaga, but I had a feeling this was all about to change. I knelt beside the lake and dropped the rock down into the murky depths. As soon as the rock touched the water, the colours filtered its way through the water. The colours bubbled to the surface and shot through the air like bullets. I looked up into the portal and noticed that the coloured bullets seemed to be healing the rift in the sky, I watched in astonishment and colour and life was breathed back into everything this land had to offer. Suddenly with a creak, our hut that once sat wrecked and ruined, was filled with swirls of magic repairing the damage and returning our home to what it once was. The looks on everyone's faces said everything, they were all full of love and smiles. Mrs Colour must have been so powerful to be able to undo the evil of Lady Malaga and keep out evil forever. I would have given anything to see the look upon her face right now. The love and kindness that this land once held had been restored and I had a feeling that this place would once again be the safe haven I had began to call home.

I sat at the edge of the lake and loved the sight of the fish leaping from the deep blue depths, I thought about the spell that I would have to use to leave this place. The only one I could think of would not work but another spell would surely work...It had to!

I looked over to the far shore on the other side of the lake and could see something flying towards me, glinting along the way. When it reached half way across the lake it split apart into twenty different colour lights, ten on each side of me. I focussed on what the lights were trying to show me and worked out that they were showing me a path across the lake and lighting the way. I looked back towards the hut and I could hear the laughter and love pouring out of all the doors and windows. Blue walked towards me and said 'You're ready Joe, it is your time. Don't look back and save this world once and for all.'

I wanted to know where this magical path led and if this was the way out of here. I summoned up all of the remaining strength I had and looked towards Blue with a longing in my heart and said 'I will be back for all of you, that is my promise.'

I started to walk along the path and as I did, I heard Blue cast out and hundreds of little floating lanterns filled with warlock light that lit the path forward. All I wanted to do was turn around but I knew that if I did, I would not face into what I knew I needed to do. I had always been bad at goodbyes and emotion filled my heart thinking of everyone that I was leaving behind. The only solace was knowing that I would be back to free them all of this place and the evil that this world had endured enough of.

Ahead of me all I could make out was the outer edge of the lake at the other side of the horizon, as I continued my walk the lanterns that Blue had conjured floated all around me and filled me with a warmth that I cherished. I reached the edge of a dark forest and knew this was the only way out, I was leaving behind all of the colour and love this land had to offer. I stepped off the end of the path and the lanterns vanished and I knew that Blue's magic could not reach me on my journey forward.

Chapter 3

THE DARK FOREST

As I continued my journey into the dark forest, I felt my ring come to life and this conjured a lantern which floated slightly in front of me. This was no ordinary lantern, it had the ability to speak and guide the caster towards its goal. I felt Ned's power slowly ebb its way back into my boots. They slowly changed before my eyes and my old friend was back with me. Ned told me that we had to find Lady Malaga's spell book as this was the only thing that would save him and his sister. I knew Ned's magic was slowly dying and knew that it was my duty to save them.

The lantern started to flicker, the light flashing on and off in a warning that something was near to us. We were suddenly plunged into darkness and the lantern spoke out inside my head 'Joe, stop walking, wait where you are and don't move a muscle.'

I came to an abrupt stop in the middle of the forest, controlling my ever-increasing breathing. Panic had started to set in with the impeding visit of whatever the lantern tried to warn me about. A sound echoed through the trees all around us, and I dashed behind one of them, hoping that I had made the right decision and that this tree wasn't a minion of Lady Malaga. Ned spoke out inside my head and told me to start climbing the tree as he knew we would all hate what was coming towards us. Without a second thought I started to climb the branches to reach the safety of the canopy above. I began to wonder why I could not cast out to defend us from whatever was coming, I totally forgot Ned could see inside my inner thoughts and told me that this forest was full of old magic that prevented other warlocks from using magic. I gave my thanks to Ned for reminding me of the rules of old magic. At the top of the canopy I could sense the runes protecting this place from other magic users. I heard the branches rustling below me and came face to face with what had been hunting us since our arrival in this dark place. Ned whispered into my thoughts that these creatures were the safe keepers of the forest known as the Dark Hunters of the Night. If they caught up with you, they would enter your darkest thoughts and manipulate your fears against you. I looked down and realised that there were thousands of them swarming all over the place, their brilliant red eyes filling the deep black with an eerie glow, these creatures were the creation of Lady Malaga, made to look like mini trees with great big hands.

I remember Blue telling me of these creatures a year ago and how he taught me how to stand against these Dark Hunters of the Night. If you stood in front of them and showed no fear then they would let you pass. They were put into the forest to guard against anyone trying to escape the ends of the earth. They stood to test you to see if you could handle the evilness that lay dormant in all of us. I knew Blue had faith in me that I could face this challenge and stop Lady Malaga once and for all. I started my descent to face this threat head on.

As I touched down on the ground, they all lined up facing me, their evil eyes sensing their next victim. One of them ran towards me and its hands grabbed me and pulled me towards its face. I tried to struggle and its grip on me became tighter and tighter. Suddenly my head became fuzzy and my body became limp in its grasp. I could feel my fears being forced from my head into my reality in front of me. My greatest fear was clowns, I could remember when my life was normal and my Mum had taken me to the circus, a clown jumped out from behind me. This is where my fear came from and has stayed with me until now. I started to shake with fear and then had another thought, telling myself that this was just my fear and it was not really in front of me. I felt my heart starting to squeeze with my irrational fear and could feel a panic attack start to set in. I began to pull myself together and repeated a mantra inside my head 'Leave now, you are not welcome here, stop clown you are not welcome here.'

The clown stopped in front of me with a sad look etched upon his cloudy blue made up face and started to fade in front of me. The fear I felt suddenly left me and I could feel my panic attack start to subside as the first dark hunter dropped me to the ground. I knew this must have been too good to be true. The Dark Hunters all took turns to grab hold of me to manipulate my fears into reality. The panic nearly took all of my strength and turned me into a quivering wreck. When I thought all was lost, the Dark Hunter dropped me to the floor and bowed its head to show that I had truly completed this test. Ned congratulated me inside my thoughts as I picked myself up and walked past the army of Dark Hunters.

I carried on my walk through the forest, I approached a tree that had been broken in half by forces not known to me. There was a sound behind the tree and a huge pair of red eyes lit up the dark around me. This dark hunter was five times the size of the others I had previously faced, he faced me and shouted 'How dare you cross my forest, you will leave at once.'

Ned shouted in my head for me to leave but I had not come this far just to turn around and leave this place. I walked closer to the Dark Hunter and he must have seen me as a threat, he leapt two feet into the air and smashed his hands on the ground. With the impact of his hands the ground started to tremble. From beneath the ground roots sprang up and trailed everywhere. Thorns shaped like little knives littered the floor, I jumped up onto the branch to stop myself falling into this trap, as I did I cast out thinking I needed the flight spell and suddenly my magic caught my fall and lifted me up into the air.

The Dark Hunter stared at me in amazement and shouted 'You can't be the one, how can you be the only one that can use magic here.' He banished his magic roots and lowered himself to the ground. The biggest Dark Hunter bowed its head at me and allowed me to continue through the dark forest. As I walked past him he said that I would find many more threats in these trees and to be on my guard. He then became as still as a block of ice, but I noticed a little blink in his eye at his surprise at who I truly was.

As I continued my walk I started to think about all those that I had left behind and if anything had changed in all of the years that I had been gone. Was Uncle Barry still tinkering in the out building making his tea of magic and if my Mum was still cooking for everyone. My thoughts moved onto my Dad and if he had managed to keep everyone safe and if the other Joe had been taught our ways of magic. I started to dread going home, what if the spell they had created the other Joe had made everyone forget about me and what if I had truly become a ghost of the past.

The night continued and it had started to feel like it had lasted forever, I knew I had to find shelter to rest and recharge myself for the challenges I would face in this forest. The wind started to pick up and a storm was brewing in the sky above me, the trees started to stir and rustle with the wind and I thought that I would use a little more magic to create a shelter for us. Ned warned me against this idea as I had already angered the forest with my use of magic and would not get away with it so easily the second time.

In the distance I could see a light flickering high up in one of the trees, this was drawing my attention towards it, I wanted to find out what it was. The wind suddenly picked up and nearly knocked me off my feet and the heavens started to open and rain started to pour. I continued my trek towards the mysterious light, and my feet got caught in the fast forming mud that the rain was creating. I started to feel my feet start to slip down further into the mud and started to worry. The more I struggled the further I sank into the mud, suddenly the great ball of light was in front of me. I tried to lift my hands to cast out and felt my arms being pulled down. The bright ball of light flew towards my face and I heard a slight thump thump of tiny wings fluttering through the air. The ball of light flew towards the ground and with a voice that was far too powerful for something so small shouted out 'Well well Joe, I can see you have got yourself into some bother.'

I replied 'Yes I have indeed, is there anything you can do to help me?'

The ball of light said 'Yes of course Joe, I am Flora.'

Nice to meet you Flora.'

She flew back into the air and waved her wand that she was carrying, the tip erupted with a dazzling spark of light that flew towards my trapped feet, the power that wand held was incredible.

'What about that then Joe, see I'm not as little as you thought, I have some great power. Would you like to see some more?' Flora said.

I was so amazed at the magic that was licking at my feet lifting me out of the mud, I had never seen anything like it, I looked down at my hand and the ring that sat snug there. I wanted a wand just like Flora and knew I needed to get one.

She noticed me look at my hand and said 'Yeah yeah, they all look at their hands when they see my wand.'

She also told me that only the fairies have the power to wield a wand and that no other person can use such power. The rules of magic were complicated to say the least.

I started to question Flora on the use of wands and the lore that there were fairies, but Flora would not give anything away. The only thing she warned me of was that if anyone else tried to use the wand it would vanish in front of them. She explained that there were not many wands left in existence.

Flora's wand was a flourish of pink and yellow and made from what looked like a delicate material not of this world. Flora spun the wand in the air to show me more magic, she created a bright white tree right in front of my eyes, it was the most beautiful tree I had ever seen apart from Mrs Colour's tree back in the ends of the world. She created an opening in the middle of the tree's bark and flew into it, as she did she called out for me to follow her.

I walked into the tree and inside was like another world, it was beautiful all around were fairies flying high in the room all with their own unique ball of light. I followed Flora through many different rooms, where there was a hive of activity. From fairy workshops creating odd fizz and popping noises to a fairy cocktail lounge with two fairies singing their hearts out to a slow haunting melody. I still could not believe that I was still in the forest when this felt like a whole new world. We got to a room where Flora showed me that I could rest as the storm outside was battering its way against the trunk of this magical fairy kingdom.

Flora spoke out to gather all of the fairies and said 'We have a new warlock with us, please welcome Joe everyone.'

All of the fairies raised their wands and showered me in flicks of magic that descended all around me. Once my welcome was complete all of the fairies got back to whatever they were doing. Flora told me to follow her and led me into a room decorated with blackboards all around me and sawn off tree trunks to sit upon, this reminded me of being back in headquarters.

Flora told me to pay attention and flew up to one of the blackboards on the wall. She moved her wand over it and it started to create shapes on the board. This happened so fast and it all came to life animating itself with Flora's magic at the very heart of it. The pictures and shapes started to play a clip of what looked like an old history clip.

The clip showed what appeared to be an older lady and she had what looked like the first and master wand of its kind. The wand she held casted a spell over little sprigs of wood and they all magically turned into other wands which were gifted to fairies far and wide. The fairies were the ones who would guard the wands as no one could ever wield the power contained within, only one family of warlocks could manipulate this kind of magic, they were the blood relatives of this old witch.

I started to believe that I could belong to this family but my heart sank when I knew this person would be Lady Malaga. It all started to make sense the woman in the clip was Lady Malaga's great grandmother. Flora told me that only a special person could reverse the spell so warlocks could wield this old power again. If the warlocks got control of this spell again it was explained to me that this would cause the destruction of magic itself, fairies had been called upon to protect and hide this secret from some power hungry warlocks.

I began to question if Lady Malaga knew of this old magic and if she did why hadn't she decided to find the wands. I asked Flora and suddenly the light that was emanating from her body dimmed in shock. This was from the mention of her name being spoken, her light came back and it was a bright red colour and her face showed an anger that I never knew Flora was capable of.

She shouted out 'She can't find out and she doesn't know, the secret was never shared with her. Everyone was told that Lady Malaga had a dark side to her. Please Joe, don't say anything you have to promise.'

I promised that I would never say anything and I dreaded to think about what the world would become if she ever found out. I still couldn't get my head around how powerful the magic was that the wands contained. A part of me wished I was never told about the wands. I started to believe that the wand Flora had belonged to the old woman in the clip. She never let the wand out of her sight, I asked how was it nobody knows about the wands and Flora explained that they were hidden from the warlocks but because I was in so much trouble in the mud earlier then she was left with no choice but to help me. I couldn't help but to keep staring at the wand in her hands, a part of me wanted to hold it to see what it would feel like in my own hands but I didn't want Flora to turn red again.

I walked away from the room as I wanted to explore this place some more, I could see a blue fairy cast out some magic. I guessed he wasn't as experienced as the other fairies as the magic he was conjuring was nowhere as powerful as the magic Flora manipulated. I introduced myself to this fairy and he told me that his name was Finley, and that he had managed to take a wand and that he should not have taken it. He continued to wave the wand through the air and nothing but a few feeble blue sparks flicked from the tip of the wand.

I really wanted to try the wand out but knew that if I tried, it would vanish from my hands. Finley waved the wand again but this time the magic that flew out was too powerful and blew the little fairy to the other side of the room. The wand hung in the air waiting for me to grab it.

I grabbed the wand and the whole room flashed with a light so bright it almost blinded me, I wrapped my fingers around the wand and felt the power crashing through my body. As soon as the magic started to flow it stopped and the wand disappeared from in front of me. I cursed that Lady Malaga would be the one to hold this wand and I could never hold it.

Finley flew away from the room and warned all the other fairies that a warlock has attempted to steal one of the sacred wands. Hundreds of fairies flew towards me, their faces bright red with anger. They all flicked their wands towards me and I was expelled from their home inside the tree. I found myself back into the cold dank woods once again.

Flora flew after me and shouted 'I can't believe you did that Joe, after all I told you and showed you. I thought you were different to all the other warlocks...Goodbye.'

She went with a flash and I was gutted to find myself alone again. I could still feel the power of the wand sparking through my fingers and could feel it call out to me. I couldn't get it out of my head and I wanted to see the wand again but the one thing I knew for sure is that I wanted to see Flora again.

I looked up into the sky and saw that the rain had stopped and the sun had begun to rise, I had completely forgotten to rest. I looked around and could see a sign. The thing with the white tree was that it was constantly moving throughout the woods and had made me miss out on any evil that I would have faced if I had never met Flora.

I walked up to the sign and it said welcome to the mountain of stones, if you wish to pass, please pull this lever. I grabbed hold of the lever and pulled, a deep rumbling sound echoed all around me and the floor dropped from under me. I found myself sliding down and down deeper into the earth. I closed my eyes and wished my descent would be over quickly.

Chapter 4

MOUNTAIN OF STONES

My slide seemed to last forever, I could feel the fresh breeze hit my face as my descent took me further and further down. I opened my eyes to see what was causing this beautiful tantalising breeze. I could see the end of the slide coming towards me faster and faster, as I reached the end of the slide I was dumped onto a patch of sand. I got up and dusted myself off and looked back to the slide and saw it disappearing. I looked around the place and there were all shapes and sizes of stones everywhere. I could see a stretch of sea in front of me and decided that was where I was going to go. I walked towards the sea and stooped down to pick up one of the stones. A voice screamed out 'Oi, put me down.'

I jumped out of my skin at the sudden voice and dropped the rock in shock, the voice spoke out again 'That hurt, why would you drop me like that.' I crouched to the floor to look at the stone that I had dropped and noticed that the stone had two eyes and a mouth I told it that I was very sorry and his eyes looked at me in disgust. I explained that I saw a beautiful rock and wanted to examine it further. It told me that he gets it a lot and loved to startle people when they picked him up. He told me that his name was Rocky, once introductions had been met, Rocky started to transform into a much bigger rock, almost half the size of me. From the middle of his body sprung a set of arms and legs. He walked me over to the water's edge and I noticed a key floating on the top of some sea foam.

'Look there, that is your way out of this place. You will need to find four other keys. No other warlock has ever made it this far.'

To get out of the ends of the earth completely, I knew I was going to have to face different parts of this magical world. This world was protected by magic unbeknown to me which stopped warlocks leaving without facing certain challenges first. I picked up the key from the sea foam and Rocky bid me good luck with my journey. He then jumped up into the air and smashed into the ground, his arms and legs gone along with his face. All that stood in Rocky's place was an old smashed up rock.

I looked down at the key and noticed a slight engraving on the reverse side. It said Yellow Box. I was intrigued to find what the yellow box was. I shouted out for Rocky and got no response, he must have left me to figure this out alone. I walked further along the edge of the sea and Ned started to cough and splutter. I looked down at my feet and noticed a nasty green moss that covered Ned. I dusted off my shoes and continued with my journey. As I continued walking the key started to vibrate in my hands, this was my only clue. When I stopped walking the key stopped vibrating. Ned then shouted out 'Look Joe, we have our first clue.'

Sure enough on the ground next to me was an arrow pointing my way ahead, I followed the arrow which pointed to a much bigger cove along the shore. I dashed for the cove and noticed a bigger arrow appear and it pointed to a large rock that had a door chiselled out of the rock with the smallest handle, I had ever seen. I grabbed hold of the handle and threw open the door.

The door was so small, there was no way I was ever going to get through it in my current state. I thought back to the time at headquarters when I had met a friend called Butter. I called out for him to join me over and over again. When I had started to lose hope that he wouldn't be able to join me in this part of the world. I heard the patter of his wings, 'Long time no see Joe, you've grown into a man, what's your mission this time?'

I told him that I needed to get out of the ends of the earth, I suddenly felt the pull of his magic over my body and I morphed into a smaller version of myself.

I jumped onto the back of Butter and he flew us through the tiny door. On the other side of the door was a bridge, the bridge was so long that you could not see the other end, it spanned a very long way. He dropped me onto the end of the bridge and wished me the best on my journey. I now knew that I could call out his name in the future if I ever needed his help again.

As I started what would be a long journey over the bridge, a bright light flew towards me. I instantly recognised this as Flora. She stopped in front of my face with panic strewn across hers. She told me that Lady Malaga had found out about the wands and that the fairies were in great danger. She told me that she did indeed have the original wand and had protected it for hundreds of years.

We got speaking about the wands as I was so intrigued by them and Flora explained that she was the one to curse the warlocks from ever touching them, as she did not want them to have the ultimate power that came with wand lore. She told me that her wand was the only one that could ever reverse the spell she had cast and that she would keep it this way as long as the wand was in her possession.

Now that Lady Malaga knew about the wands, I knew she would stop at nothing to get this power for herself, she wanted the power to be able to kill warlocks once and for all. Things had taken a turn for the worst and I knew that Flora and I were now both being hunted. You could feel that a battle was on its way as Lady Malaga was hungry for the ultimate power. I would stop at nothing to make sure this would not happen and to protect Flora with my own life.

Flora decided to sit on my shoulder and told me that she would be carefully watching over me and laughed when she threatened to turn me into a frog if I attempted any funny business. Flora pointed out something shining through the bridge further up ahead. We ran over and it was another key very similar to the one I had already possessed. We reached down for the key but it was wedged into the wood, I struggled to pull it out of the wood, it would not budge at all. Flora took it upon herself to try, she waved the wand and uttered a few words in a language I did not recognise and sparks flew all around us. The wood blew apart into little pieces and the key flew up into the air, I cast out myself to lift myself into the air to catch the second key. Something took over Flora and her once blue eyes turned a nasty shade of green, she pointed her wand at the floating key and a shot of power hit the key causing it to spiral higher into the air. I flew higher into the air and caught the key, I allowed myself to come back to the ground, I looked over at Flora and saw that her eyes still had the evil shade of green, her mouth twisted into a sneer and whispered 'You think you're stronger than I am do you?'

She then flew up into the air and waved her wand again, the sparks flew from the wand hundreds of times faster than before and so much brighter. She aimed the sparks directly at me, I ran further along the bridge as Flora's attacks rained down on the bridge, blowing apart different pieces of the bridge. Suddenly the attacks stopped and Flora dropped to the ground, her eyes closed and her breathing slowed down. I ran over to her and as I did she opened her eyes and they again were the normal shade of blue. The wand had fallen from her hand and was lying next to her, my fingers itched to pick it up but I had learnt my lesson from before. She told me that her head was hurting and explained that this had happened to her previously and that she could not remember anything from the times when it did happen to her. After a while her wings start to twitch and she flew to pick up the wand again.

The wand had changed Flora for sure but I needed to know why. A noise coming from the sea disturbed our thoughts, we ran over to the edge of the sea to see what was causing the noise, the waves started to crash against the shore. Suddenly the sea calmed right down until a massive explosion of power in the air stirred our attention. In the air Lady Malaga cackled as she descended right in front of us. She shouted 'Thanks for finding the fairies Joe, I've been looking for them for years. That little show from your fairy friend was all for me.'

She then looked upon Flora and saw the wand in her hand, her face filled with rage and shouted 'Give me that wand or you and your fairies will live to regret it.'

Flora was not taking any of Lady Malaga's nonsense and pointed her wand directly at her in the clouds. A massive beam of light hit Lady Malaga directly in the chest and the smirk was knocked off her face. This was the only time I had seen a weakness of Lady Malaga. Flora took another shot at Lady Malaga and she disappeared, the sea started to bubble up and a foul voice filled the air 'You think you can stop me do you, if you won't give me that wand, I will snatch it from your fingers.'

The feeling of a curse flew all around us and Flora told me that Lady Malaga had cursed us both to make our journey from this place that ever more harder. All of her minions would now be after us. Flora looked at me and concern washed over her face, I knew that we were both in a lot of danger and the curse would linger until Lady Malaga was defeated. Flora told us that we needed to head to the lakes which was not much further ahead of us.

I followed Flora as she showed me to the lakes, she warned me of the curse that had been cast over us, that anything could happen. She started to explain that there were mermaids in the lakes and that they would help in any way that they could. She also warned that the mermaids could be dangerous and that we must always watch our backs. Just ahead I could see the lakes. The bright blue of the sky reflected in the mesmerising lakes. Suddenly an eruption of colour filled the lakes and changed them from the bright blue colour to a dusty purple red. The curse that Lady Malaga had cast was causing this change. What once was lush green grass turned into a crop of razor sharp needles. Flora swiped her wand through the air and created a path above the needles for us to safely pass.

The needles started to smash the underside of the path and created little holes in Flora's magic. She shouted out that her magic would not last much longer. I cast out and I flew upwards from the path and Flora came to sit on my shoulder just as her magical path cracked under the pressure of attack and blew up. I circled my ring around us both and created a protection bubble, the needles bounced straight off my bubble. Flora reinforced my protection bubble with her wand, as she did I could feel her magic entwine with mine and my spell became a hybrid force that radiated energy.

We continued flying through the air protected by our powers combined and flew over a patch of mud. The mud sprung to life and a hand crashed over our protective bubble trying to pull us to the ground, Flora tried to cast from inside our bubble but her wand did not seem to work from within my shield.

When I thought all was lost and that we would be pulled under the mud, a bright blue energy orb flew towards us. The orb surrounded our bubble and pulled us away from the mouth that had opened up in the centre of the mud. Flora shouted out 'Misty what are you doing here?'

The blue orb materialised and another fairy flew next to us and smirked at us 'I've come to save you, I thought you both needed an extra pair of wings.'

Flora was so happy to see Misty, they hugged and spoke in a strange fairy language. I cleared my throat and they both started to laugh. Flora told Misty that we all were in great danger from Lady Malaga and her curse and ordered Misty to return to the fairy sanctuary. Misty refused and demanded a fairy battle between herself and Flora. 'If I win, then I'll stay and if you win, I will go home.' Misty said.

I could see that Flora did not like this idea but gave in, I watched the two fairies come face to face and then flew apart from each other. Flora spoke out to me and told me that the aim of a fairy battle was to change the colour of your opponent's wings, the first fairy to change the other's wings three times would win. The battle began and both fairies fired their wands at each other, the magic spells smashed together between the fairies and created a flash of light so bright, I thought my eyes would burn, this had to be brighter than the sun. The magic started to flick towards Misty and hit her wings, they changed from blue to a dusty shade of pink… Flora had scored the first point.

Misty laughed at Flora and said 'I let you have that one.' Without further warning Misty flicked her wand and the streak of light hit Flora's wings and then changed colour. Flora got angry and flew higher into the air, her cheeks tinged with red, you could practically see the steam pouring from her ears. Flora cast her wand towards Misty and the force of the flash of light was so powerful, Misty face hit the ground. Her wings changed colour again and Flora cheered with her second point of the battle.

The two fairies continued throwing bolts of light at each other from their wands. One rogue light hit a tree and smashed it in half. One half came flying right towards me and I drew a protection circle around me. The battle was getting nasty as Misty kept flinging her wand all over the place, the spells hit everything in its path. Flora shouted at Misty to stop as she was getting nastier and nastier and that the evil within could take over at any minute. At the mention of this Misty flew straight for Flora and managed to sneak a flash of light and it hit Flora's wings, they changed colour again giving Misty her second point of the battle.

Flora was so angry that she made a snatching motion with her hand, her wand flew out of her hand and flew after Misty. It was like the wand had a mind of its own and chased Misty through the sky. Misty flew higher and higher into the sky and dodging out of the way of the magic erupting out of the end of Flora's wand.

Misty was firing back at Flora's wand to protect herself, Flora cackled and called out to her wand and it stopped dead in the air, her wand started to multiply and fire streams of light all towards Misty. Misty shouted out 'Ok ok, stop you win.'

Misty flew down to the ground beside me along with Flora, Flora recalled her wand and all of the multiplied wands disappeared. Flora dropped beside Misty and Misty dropped her wand to the floor in an action that said she conceded the battle. Flora started to drop her wand. Misty started to laugh and a beam of light hit Flora's wings and they changed colour. 'You fell for it again Flora, that was the wand spell.'

'You sneaky little fairy Misty, you certainly have fairy courage.'

Misty came over and gave Flora a hug and explained that she really wanted to help and said she had to play dirty as she knew that she would never win against Flora playing by the rules.

I lowered my protection spell as the two fairies started to laugh their heads off at each other. Misty turned to me and asked if I was heading to the lakes. I told her that I was and she told me that on her way there the mermaids had tried to attack her and that they must have changed when Lady Malaga had created her curse. Flora told Misty that she would look after us and that she will be safe.

We all started to make our way to the lakes, Flora and Misty started to talk again in their fairy language and English at the same time. I picked up that Misty thinks there is a fairy within the fairy kingdom working for Lady Malaga in secret. Misty could not work out which fairy it was but knew she needed to come and tell Flora straight away. I made them a promise that I would find out who this fairy was and would make sure that no other fairies would be harmed. They both smiled at me and pointed their wands straight at my heart. I felt a warming sensation as they both bestowed a gift upon me, the gift was the knowledge of the fairies and I would be able to speak their language from now on.

I hoped the fairies would be ok and Misty explained that before she left the fairies, to come and help us, that they were getting ready to make sure evil could not take them over. I thought about Flora's wand, the most powerful fairy wand ever made and hoped that the other fairies would be fine without it.

We continued walking for the next hour or so and Ned called out inside my head again. 'Stop Joe, I'm all wet and getting cold.'

I looked down and could see that I was walking through shallow water, I heard Flora cry out for us all to look behind us, I spun around so quick that I made myself slightly dizzy. A thick fog had started to crawl over the mountain of stones, this started to block out the sun beating down on us. The fog started to chase us as we continued our dash to the cursed lakes.

Chapter 5

THE CURSED LAKES

I suddenly felt my boots fill with water and looked down at Ned to find the water from the lakes had reached where we were standing. I began to think how odd this was as we were still a few feet away from the nearest lake.

I felt the water swish over my boots and start trailing up my leg, this felt odd and like something peculiar was at work here. Flora and Misty shouted out at the same time 'Quick get off the ground, these are the cursed lakes.'

I cast out and flew into the air alongside Misty and Flora, as I did blue light surrounded the water on the ground and a figure rose from the depths of the water with a sinister presence about it. Misty explained that this was a member of the water army from the cursed lakes. These had been magicked into existence to protect the borders to this world.

Suddenly more of the army erupted from the water obviously looking for the people who had disturbed their watery slumber. Flora told me that the army would grab you and cover your body in water, slowly working its way towards your mouth to cut off your valuable air supply. This army came from an old and powerful spell book many centuries ago, and this curse has lasted the test of time. I knew we had to stay in the air until these eerie figures had passed and it was safe enough for us to be back on the ground. We had to make our way across the cursed lakes and I knew this was going to be a difficult task as we would have to face the lake army and also the dreaded mermaids.

I looked down and saw that the figures had started to descend back into the water, as they did I released the magic that was keeping me in the air and touched softly onto the ground. Almost instantly I felt the water creeping its was back up my legs. I cast and flew back into the air. This task seemed impossible, how the hell would we ever cross the lakes with these figures watching our every move. As we were flying through the air, Flora told us of a secret passageway through the lakes that would protect us from the water army, I could tell there was something she was not letting on. I started to think that this passageway was where the mermaids would live and who knows what other nasties that this place had to offer.

As we flew through the air, I had an idea that I believed would work. I explained to Flora and Misty that I would touch the ground, and that would give them the time to reach the passageway, and once they got there, they could cast out their magic and pull me towards them. I knew this came with plenty of risks as I did not want to fall victim to the water army and have my breath snatched from me forever. Flora knew a spell that could help us achieve this goal but was very apprehensive of using it because when it was used it had the tendency to go rogue. We all agreed that this was the best plan we could come up with in the short amount of time that we had.

I flew towards the ground and stopped using my magic which allowed me to press my feet firmly on the ground. Within seconds I felt the water enter my boots and start lapping at my legs. I shouted out to Misty and Flora 'Go we haven't got the time for you to float around staring.'

I looked over and saw that Flora and Misty had made it to the passageway. I heard Flora cast out as the water started to touch the base of my neck. I waited patiently and nothing happened. The water is now touching the outside of my throat. I started to panic right as a spell hit me in the middle of my chest. The water that had covered me started to get warm, I started to glow and looked down at what was causing this to happen. My arms and legs had started to vanish and the next thing I knew was that

I was beside Misty and Flora with the water army trailing behind us.

'It worked, it worked Flora.' Misty shouted out in a voice full of cheer and a huge grin plastered onto her face.

'I guess it did.' Replied Flora smirking at herself.

Right in front of us was an ancient door that had water running all around it, Flora told us that once we went through there was no returning, as this door was a one way passage only and the only other way out was at the end of the cursed lakes.

The passageway we were going to go through went under the lakes and we would have to cast a bubble of breathing which would allow us to breathe normally under the immense pressure of the water above us. Flora explained how to complete the spell and as we did, a bubble came up and wrapped itself around my mouth and nose. I breathed in and started to cough with this new sensation that was passing through my lungs. After a moment of spluttering, I started to get used to the sensation and told the two fairies that we should get going. Flora banged on the door with her wand twice and the door slowly creaked open, and water started to leak through the gaps and flood around our feet. We all ran forward and pressed through the veil of this door, I panicked slightly and closed my eyes. After a minute or so I opened them and my mouth dropped open in amazement.

In front of me was the most amazing sight my eyes had ever had the pleasure of looking at. Every coloured fish you could imagine swam before me, crabs lazily crawling along the lake bed and sea shoots that shot green lights out of the ends of them. I looked behind me to look at the door and found that it had vanished completely.

Misty pointed towards a shadow making its way towards us, and shouted for us to be on our guard. Flora and Misty readied their wands and I raised my ring, I looked over to Flora's wand and felt the familiar pull towards it, I wished in that moment that it was me holding the wand and not her. We carried on making our way towards the shadow that was slowly advancing on us. Flora told Misty to stay back and casted from her wand, a wall materialised out of nowhere and then vanished. I cast out with my ring and a sheet of mirrored glass appeared, I thought that it would hide us for a moment, Misty shouted 'Good one Joe.'

Flora didn't seem bothered by the attempt at all and I knew this was because my spell had worked when hers had not. My spell had seemed to be working when all of a sudden the mirror started to disappear, it seemed like our magic did not work very well under the cursed lakes.

We reached the edge of an abyss and all staggered backwards to stop us from falling, the shadow was leering towards us from the depths within. Flora seemed to think that her magic was the best and cast out again, her spell hit a rock on the lake bed and made it explode into thousand of pieces, this caught the attention of the shadow and it marched towards us even faster. I heard a slight cry out and saw Misty start to fall down into the abyss, a piece of the rock had shot into her abdomen.

I dived down to save Misty but as I did my bubble kept pushing me back upwards, I only then realised that my magic had limits down here and would not work if I pushed it too far. Flora told me the only way to save Misty was for her to cast away her bubble and dive down into the abyss. Flora looked at me with tears in her eyes and said 'Joe I'm sorry I have no other choice.'

Before I could stop her, Flora cast out and I was pushed away from her, Flora waved her wand in front of her face and the bubble disappeared from her mouth and nose. Flora took a swan's leap off the edge and dived deeper and deeper into the abyss. I jumped in after her but my bubble forced me back to the edge and would not let me go after my two fairy friends. Suddenly darkness took over the forms of Misty and Flora and I couldn't see them any more. I shouted out for both of them but heard nothing in return.

I started to panic and thought of any way I could save them when a flash of light pierced through the darkness. Misty was flying back towards me with a blue light trailing behind her, the force of Flora's magic doing what I thought was not possible. Misty came beside me and I checked her over, the shard of rock had vanished and she looked fully healed. I pulled her tiny body towards me, as I hugged her I asked where Flora was and Misty's eyes started to leak tears at the obvious misery that was about to unfold. I looked over the edge of the abyss and called out Flora's name time and time again but to no avail. I heard Misty shout out and I shot around to see her wand start to disappear, once it had fully vanished, Flora's wand materialised into Misty's waiting hand and a shot of sparks noted a new owner had taken a hold of the most powerful fairy wand this world had ever seen.

I looked Misty in the eye and tears started to stream down my face, I knew that I must go after my Flora and save her from the depths of this place. I told Misty my idea and she was not happy and said she could not face another one of her friends sacrificing themselves. I told her that this is what good friends do for each other and if we didn't save Flora, then the other fairies would be heartbroken. I explained to Misty that I knew a spell that could re-animate the dead and bring them back to life and that it was a spell I had learnt a very long time ago. I told her that if I succeeded I would flash a ball of purple light towards Misty to make her bring us back to safety. Misty agreed but told me that she didn't think this was the best plan that I had ever had. I took a running jump off the ledge and as I did made my bubble surrounding my mouth and nose, that was providing me much needed oxygen disappear. I dived deeper into the dark and could see shadow after shadow gather together. I came to an abrupt stop and started to run my hands over the bottom of this part of the lake. I frantically searched for the feel of Flora, I conjured up some warlock light and suddenly her body appeared a few metres in front of me. I dashed over to her and reminded myself to slow down a little as I needed to conserve my oxygen. I raised my hands in front of me and remembered the resurrection spell, I uttered the incantation inside my head and my ring glowed and then radiated power towards Flora's body. I concentrated and suddenly I noticed the rise and fall of Flora's chest, had I really pulled this spell off and brought another creature back to life? I picked up her fragile body and wrapped her in the crook of my arm and shot up a ball of light to Misty to signal her to bring us back up to where she waited. We waited for a few more seconds and I felt my oxygen supplies start to dwindle, when I had lost hope an almighty spark pierced the blackness and wrapped a bubble around us both, I breathed in fresh oxygen, my lungs screaming out in relief. I looked down and noticed that we were being pulled up by the wand Misty clung to with dear life. As we neared where Misty was, Flora's eyes flitted open and she said 'Joe thank you for saving me, without you I would have been doomed. When you feel life ebbing away from you, you really think about things and I promise you that I will be a better fairy from now on.'

With that her wings started to glow brightly, we came up to where Misty was and Flora flew over to her and gave her a big hug. 'I'm sorry Misty, I love you very much but please can I have my wand back?' Flora asked

Misty returned the wand to Flora and then Flora cast out a spell from the wand, the wand seemed to glow brighter than ever and it recognised being returned to its true master. Suddenly another wand appeared and Misty grabbed it, a shower of sparks erupted around us as magic user and wand were reunited for the final time.

We continued across the cursed lakes with our breathing bubbles intact, we flew over the abyss and left the horror of what had happened previously behind us. I began to think about how amazing magic was because I had just successfully brought someone back from the brink of death. I knew for sure Lady Malaga could never know of this spell or get her dirty hands on the fairies wands. As we continued our journey a shadow flicked in front of us and I swore that it looked like a tail. Flora told me that the mermaids had finally caught up with us. She told me that she and Misty were small enough to hide and that I should transform my legs into a tail to offer myself some protection. She slammed her magic into me and I could feel my legs snap together and scales start to pop up all over. Ned shouted out in my head 'Oi, I don't want to be a tail, thank you very much.'

Flora laughed and said 'Sorry Ned, you don't really have a choice.'

I spun my head around and said to Flora 'Wait, you can hear Ned as well.'

She laughed at me and nodded. They both hid behind some rocks but told me they would be keeping a close eye on me. Misty cast a spell and said they would always keep in touch as her wand would be our communication device. I swam around testing my new tail out and spun around as fast as I could. Suddenly a voice entered my head and Flora said 'Be careful Joe, you're making too much noise and causing too many distractions, be careful.'

Ned started to tell me off as well and it started to feel like I was being ganged up on. I finally worked out how to use my new body and looked out in front of me. I noticed the shadows that Flora spoke about, I swam away from them but couldn't move fast enough, the shadows wrapped around me and pulled me back. A shout that caused me to jump out of my scales sounded out 'Unidentified mer-person identify yourself.'

I had no idea what I was going to say when I heard Flora instruct me to say that I was Olly the merman, who was here to collect the sacred merman shell. I took her advice and said exactly that. Suddenly the shadows disappeared and let me pass. Misty and Flora caught up with me and told me that the shadows would report anything that had happened to the nobility of the mermaids and that they would soon catch up with us.

We carried on swimming for what felt like forever, suddenly a huge crab crunched his claws in front of our faces. Misty flung herself in front of us and cast out from her wand. Nothing happened to the crab and again the claw smashed down on top of the wand and knocked it clearly out of Misty's hands. Misty stood there shell shocked as her wand dropped to the lake bed. Flora threw herself in front of me and fired some huge blue sparks from the end of her wand. Suddenly the crab started to shrink until Flora could pick it up in her own hands. Misty went down to retrieve her wand and gave Flora the most horrid stare. I had a feeling that other fairies hated each other when they outdid each other. Once Misty had retrieved her wand Flora spoke to me that we needed to find the sacred merman shell as that was our only way out of the cursed lakes.

Suddenly a massive gush of water all around us pulled us further along, it felt like we were being sucked through a tunnel, Flora told me that this was close to where we needed to head. Misty shouted out that this was her wand's way of making sure we headed in the right direction.

Flora said that we were heading into the realm of the protectors, and that this realm would be where we could find the sacred shell and escape the cursed lakes forever. The protectors do not like unwanted visitors and that it could be a very dangerous place to be. The twists and turns of this tunnel were getting smaller and we dashed past them quicker and quicker. Flora shouted out for me to reach out and get ready, suddenly I felt a dull thud against my hands, I looked down and saw that a shell with an inscription of a merman was there. Was this really the sacred shell of the merman? The shell cracked open and inside a bubble wrapped in a tangle of seaweed lay waiting to be claimed. I touched the bubble and it shot up my fingers towards my face. The breathing bubble returned and slowly the scales that were on my tail started to drop and fade away. The two fairies cheered and clapped as I was returned to normal. Ned spoke out in my head 'Well done Joe, I thought I would be stuck smelling like fishy feet forever.'

We continued along the trail and Flora told us to be on our guard, rumours had been flying around the fairy kingdom that a warlock had once come down here and had never returned. I asked his name in case I had ever known of him at headquarters and the fairies laughed and said 'No Joe, this was way before your time, we believe his name was Fred.'

I wondered if I would ever meet this Fred character as we continued flowing through our escape tunnel. Suddenly there was a flash of light and Flora shouted for us to brace. I looked around in a daze and could not make out Misty, Flora was the only fairy left. I asked Flora where Misty was, as I did the tunnel came to an abrupt end and I was pushed through a veil towards the realm of the protectors. I took a deep breath when another flash came and Flora too disappeared. I whooshed through another veil so fast that my cheeks stared to wobble, I closed my eyes as I continued my crossing suddenly my eyes were flung open and I could see all around me.

Chapter 6

THE PROTECTORS

I flew into the air from the end of the tunnel and cast the flying spell to balance myself and not plunge back into the water from which I came. There were no signs of Misty or Flora anywhere, I continued my flight forward and suddenly saw a bank of land jutting up from the water. I flew towards the land and softly touched down, I looked around and called out for Misty and Flora, no reply came from either of them and I started to wonder if I was all alone. I spotted a long narrow path that was etched through the barren landscape, in the distance I saw one of the rocks that littered the pathway start to move. I continued walking up the path closer to the rock, it stopped moving and sank down under the path. I came across another stone and it did exactly the same as the first, I didn't think anything about it and continued walking on the path. I heard a distant rumbling and felt a tremor through my boots. Ned spoke out and said 'Something isn't right Joe, be careful.'

Suddenly the path started to crumble and fall into a cavernous pit that had formed under the path. I conjured up my magic and felt the power flow through my ring. It felt like a dull ache as the power that would usually form a flying spell failed to transpire. Why would my magic not work and why was I trapped on this forsaken path that would end up being my doom.

Then a sinister laughter filled the air and I looked up into the blue sky and watched as black smoke start to litter the beautiful sky. I knew that the dreaded Lady Malaga was chasing me down even here, I looked back into the sky and watched intently as the shadow of black swirled around and made a dart for the very path that I was on. It smacked into the remaining part of the path and its full force of power trembled the whole ground. The shadow now on the ground started to form into a shape similar to that of a human but a lot taller. I knew what stood in front of me was what they called a protector, it had a long black cloak with a hood attached that covered its face. It cast a ball of undiluted magic straight at me, the force of the magic ripping up everything in its path, then a venomous voice spoke out 'You are a fool to think you would ever get past me, what are you doing here and make your answer quick before this path becomes your tomb.'

The path at this point was working its way around my body, building a wall around me, getting taller by the minute. I had to do something or this is where I would become no more. I shouted out to the protector and said 'I mean you no harm, I have lost two friends both who belong to the fairy race and I am trying to get out of the ends of the earth and face Lady Malaga.'

As soon as I mentioned Lady Malaga's name, the magic that was whipping around my ears creating my tomb exploded into tiny little pieces, the protector vanished and I whipped my head around frantically searching for anything that would cause this mysterious happening. I suddenly heard the rustling of wings and almost jumped with glee at the sight of my two fairy friends. Flora shot pure power from the end of her wand straight at me to save me from falling into the pit under the path. She smirked at me and said 'Come on Joe, what are you waiting for, come with us.'

I cast out and flew up to meet Flora and Misty, still in shock at what had just happened. I hugged both of them and pure happiness filled my heart that came with us being reunited. We flew towards the ground and Flora told me that what I had encountered was indeed a protector, I asked why my magic did not work against them and she told me that they had control over everything and could manipulate everything even our own magic.

As we were flying through the air, the fairies thought it was a good idea to have a fairy race to see who the fastest was. I think they forgot the real reason that we were here, it wasn't to play stupid fairy games it was to get out of this end of the earth once and for all. I shouted out to Flora and Misty to stop playing these games and to start being nice to one another, but as you can imagine that fell on deaf ears. The fairies continued racing and I struggled to keep up with both of them. I shot out sparks of warning from my ring to get the attention of both fairies, Misty did not like that one little bit and the redness overtook her face once again. She caught me off guard and flung a magic spell towards me that caused me to plummet to the ground, I cast out when I was mere inches from smacking my face and flew back up towards the fairies. Misty was laughing hysterically like she was a pure loon. Pure anger shot through my body and out of my ring and clipped Misty's wings, that wiped the grin off her face and she struggled to regain control over her wings. Flora was just watching absent mindedly whilst we had our own little battle. Misty waved her wand and fireworks erupted behind her that sent her flying back up towards me. She charged towards me flinging her magic at me, spell after spell I deflected back towards her. One of her spells managed to graze my shoulder and I was frozen unable to call upon my magic or wriggle out of this magical hold. She came towards me yet again but this time Flora intervened and came thundering over to us, a magical barrier erected between us.

Flora shouted at Misty 'Stop this right now, you need to control your temper, I've had it with you.'

Misty lifted her wand to attempt to strike at Flora but she was too fast, Flora lazily flicked her wand and created a colourful bubble that was sent flying towards Misty and sucked her inside. Flora flew to the bubble and whispered to it 'Send her home and keep her safe, teach her a lesson and do it with haste.'

Misty was screaming from within the bubble saying that she was sorry and this wouldn't happen again but Flora was not having any of it, the bubble vanished with a pop and carried Misty back to fairyland. Flora turned to me and said 'You're an idiot to think you can take on a fairy, why would you do that Joe?'

I apologised and said I would never try anything like that again, Flora smiled at me and said 'Make sure you don't Joe, I won't be as kind on you.'

She went on to explain that she had conjured a fairy bubble and it had one purpose, that was to transport misbehaving fairies back home to safety. Nothing could penetrate the bubble as this was created with magic conjured from the very first fairy wand and only Flora had the power to create them.

Flora waved her wand and I became unfrozen, I stretched out my muscles and was grateful as my body had started to hurt from being kept in one position for so long. Flora and I continued flying through this place making idle conversation, Flora was worried that Misty would try and turn the other fairies against her and come after her. It was such a shame to hear that Flora could not trust Misty any more and had had to take such drastic action. I began to wonder if the other fairies were hungry for the power that Flora held and if these fights were a common thing in fairyland. I would protect her at all costs, I knew that ultimately I would need to take the wand. I had to come up with a plan that would allow me to take the wand from Flora to save her once and for all from the other fairies and Lady Malaga.

We reached an area where we could land, it felt like we had been flying for hours. We had passed lakes so vast, I thought they would never end and then we must have passed hundreds of black shadows which Flora told me were the protectors, I wondered why they couldn't see us in the air.

As we landed Flora cast a protection spell that would ward us against the protectors, this would make sure that they couldn't manipulate anything to hurt us. Flora turned to me and said 'The protectors know everything that happens in their lands and will be waiting to strike.'

Flora continued to fire magic from her wand and I could see her energy dim, I knew that she could not keep up with the complexity of magic without needing to rest, she looked at me feebly 'Joe, I can only hold this spell for so long, you need to be ready for when my magic starts to fail. Remember they will use your magic against you so be clever and out think them. Once my magic fails I will be wrapped in the rest bubble so I can rest and recuperate.'

It felt like my heart was beating out of my chest with the sheer panic that had started to flood my body. I understood what Flora was saying but that did not make what I was about to face any easier. I began to think of a plan and looked back over to Flora and could see the magic coming from her wand tip being pulled back towards her and forming a bubble around her, I had never seen anything like this before, was Flora and her wand really capable of creating two spells at once?

With a dull thud, Flora's magic stopped and she became suspended in her bubble and fell backwards into what I could only imagine was the fairy sleep. In the distance I could make out the shadows rushing towards me, I knew this was the protectors come to protect the land they thought belonged to them. The ground started to rumble and then started to rip apart with the sheer power the protectors carried. I heard a small voice shout out at me 'Quick, get yourself over here.'

I looked over my shoulder and there was a man standing, waving his arms like a crazy person shouting 'Move yourself, get here now.'

I ran towards the man and as I passed him, I saw that he cast a spell towards the protector that caused everything to freeze. The man grabbed my arm and everything went dark, I could feel a warm tingling work its way up my arm. Suddenly everything started to come clearer and I noticed that I was in a hut, the man's voice rang out and said 'Fancy a cuppa lad?'

I looked around my surroundings and noticed the man standing in the background of the hut. He had long matted brown hair that looked like it hadn't been washed for a long time and a brown coat that touched his massive brown boots. The coat had moth holes everywhere like they had feasted their way through the leather. I was in total shock, one minute I was facing certain trouble against the protectors and now I was here being offered a cup of tea in a hut from an unknown man.

'I'm Fred by the way, and a thank you would be nice for just saving your warlock butt.'

'Sorry Fred, nice to meet you, I'm just in shock, you're the warlock everyone thinks is dead.' I replied

'Yes Yes, you don't have to say it, I'm the one everyone thinks is dead, I've come close a few times but I'm certainly alive and kicking at the moment.'

So this was the Fred that the fairies spoke about back in the cursed lakes. I was wondering if I would ever meet him and now here I was standing in his hut. I wanted to know some more about Fred and if this was also his time to leave this place and if I would be the one to help him. I asked Fred where Flora was and he told me that he had pulled her bubble inside and that she was still resting in the other room. Fred handed me the promised cup of tea which sat boiling over his open fireplace.

I started to drink and Fred settled on a stool just in front of the fire, he gestured for me to sit beside him to get warm. I sat down and he asked why I was here. I told him everything from being in headquarters to being cast out to the ends of the earth. He told me that his story was very similar and that he had tried to escape many times but failed. I wanted to prove to Fred that I would be the one to escape and take him with me. He told me he found us by chance earlier on, he felt a pull of magic that he hadn't felt for years. The wand magic must call out to all magical folk and that was how he found

Flora and I. Fred went on to say that he only had power to escape from the protectors and not to stand against them and this is how we got back to his hut.

Fred threw more wood on the fire and it became white hot, I thought I saw a face in the flames and double glanced to make sure I wasn't seeing things. Sure enough in the flames was Lady Malaga. I felt myself being hypnotised by the flames' movement and must have crawled closer to the fire. I came to with Fred pulling me away. It was at this point her poisonous voice filled the hut around us 'Well well Joe, I can see you have been busy and that you are coming after me, how about a little burn to brighten up your day?'

The fire started to crackle and burn even brighter and her laughter emanated from the walls. She walked out of the flames, her black dress being licked by the fire behind her. She raised her hand and manipulated the flames to rise higher into the air and latch onto the hut's roof causing it to catch alight and blaze. Fred shouted that we had to get out, I dashed into the other room to save Flora, I shouted for her to wake up. Flora's eyes shot open and the bubble that she was in expanded around the hut to protect it from the damage that Lady Malaga was causing. We both dashed into the main part of the hut and could see Lady Malaga battling against the magic Flora had summoned. Lady Malaga dropped her hand and shot up into the sky straight through the roof. She snatched her hand away from her body which caused a lightning bolt to crash against the roof of the hut, the walls started to tremble with the damage that was being caused.

I ran outside and shouted up to the evil witch to leave Fred's home alone, she looked over at me and started to laugh saying 'Joe you are indeed a very brave warlock, but that will only get you so far.'

Again she cast another lightning bolt towards the hut and this time the power held within the bolt caused the hut to explode into little pieces that littered the ground around us. It was amazing that no one was hurt. Lady Malaga came back towards the ground and her dress unfurled and ropes began to fly towards Fred. He cast out several times to try and stop the ropes but his magic was just not strong enough. The ropes wrapped themselves around Fred and ripped off his warlock ring and let it fall to the ground. As the ring hit the ground it shattered which echoed all around us. Lady Malaga laughed at her accomplishment and said 'Fred my dear old friend, how nice it is to see you after all this time. How dare you think you could make a stand against me. Just like before, you will never see the light of day again.'

Before he could reply or either of us could do anything to help him, his body started to turn to stone. Flora shot out of nowhere and flung some wild magic towards Lady Malaga that caused her to drop him to the ground, her spell not enough to completely turn Fred to stone. Lady Malaga turned into a cloud of black smoke which shot mini bolts of lightening towards Flora, with a casual flick of her wand the bolts froze in the air for a second and then vanished. Her foul voice entered the clearing around us and said she would be waiting for us, that was if death didn't claim us in this place first. Flora was beside me in a shot and muttered an incantation that I did not know and Fred's legs began to turn back into what they were before Lady Malaga had attempted to turn him to stone. She flew over to where his ring was destroyed and circled her wand over it. Believe it or not the ring's pieces flew up into the air and remoulded themselves. I looked over at Fred and could see that the ring had reappeared on his finger.

Flora spoke out and explained to us both that her wand can do extraordinary things but if Lady Malaga had succeeded in turning Fred to stone then it would have been game over for him. I wished I had known Flora at the time Mr Fire was turned to stone and then maybe she could have helped him. I was beginning to get a little bored with Lady Malaga's relentless malice towards us and knew I would beat her one way or another.

Fred thanked Flora for everything she had done for him and told us not to worry about his hut. We watched on with amazement as he cast out and all the pieces floated up into the air and reassembled themselves. Fred said 'Now for my next party trick, watch this.'

He cast out again and the whole hut became the size of a golf ball. He picked it up and placed it inside one of the pockets of his coat. I could not believe my eyes, that Fred had the power to be able to take his hut wherever he want. He told us that he would make Lady Malaga pay for what she had just done and it filled me with a warmth knowing that I had another ally in Fred.

Fred told us to make tracks towards the Old Lands which were not that far away, he told both Flora and I that we would be safe with him at our sides. Flora burst out giggling and corrected Fred by saying 'No Fred, you both will be safe with me at your sides.'

We walked through what felt like a huge forest and luckily for us were not bothered by any more protectors, maybe Lady Malaga scared them away with her presence but I thought we were so lucky not to have them chasing us again. I looked over to my right and noticed etched onto one of the tree trunks was a very old sign that pointed just ahead of us with the words Old Lands.

Chapter 7

OLD LANDS

I walked up to the sign and saw that a spider was hanging off it, dangling from a thick strand of web, I could have sworn that the spider winked at me whilst I was looking at it. I suddenly started to laugh as the thought of Ned being turned into fins entered my head, he was whinging and moaning the whole time as he hated water, Ned spoke out in my head to stop laughing at him. Fred came up behind me and tapped me on the shoulder, I turned around and Fred told me to be aware of the spiders, he said they acted like they were your friends to try and lure you into their hideout. Here they would cast the spider curse on you and the mother of all spiders would take your ring off you so she could take your powers all for herself. They wanted to take over the world, a shiver ran down my spine at the thought of the world teeming with spiders.

Flora piped up with her snooty attitude and said 'Well I think that's the biggest load of rubbish I've ever heard in my whole fairy life.'

'Hahahaha why did you have to ruin my fun.' Replied Fred.

Thank god for that, I was so glad that it was a joke, I had started to panic, I wiped the bead of sweat that had rolled down my forehead. Fred started to laugh at Flora and she did not look happy at all. She waved her wand and a huge spider materialised out of nowhere, Fred let out a scream and cast himself into the air to get away from the spider. I did the same and both Fred and I floated up into the air, Flora started to laugh so much that she lost her balance and fell to the ground. Flora's face turned a beetroot shade of purply red with embarrassment, she flicked her wand and the spider disappeared. Fred and I flew back to the ground and Fred ran over to help Flora, she pushed him off her and cast a million tiny spiders to start crawling over Fred's body. He waved his hand over his body with a shout and all the spiders turned into grains of rice that dropped to the ground. I shouted out to the pair of them 'Enough, we have to work with each other and not against each other.'

Fred and Flora apologised and hugged each other. Fred told us to get a move on so he could set up his hut and we could all have a nice cup of tea and also sort out food for us all. Flora seemed quiet after her performance but I thought she had forgiven Fred. I would have to have a chat with Flora as we could not keep risking her little outbursts of magic like this, as it could put us in grave danger. After all she was holding the world's strongest wand, I wanted that wand more and more and Ned's voice popped into my head 'I want that wand as well Joe, it could save me and my sister. Each day that passes I can feel her slipping away.'

We carried on walking trying to find the perfect spot to set Fred's hut up, he kept muttering to himself mentioning something was not right, it was like the hut was speaking to him and letting him know if it could be set up there. I looked up to the sky and could see some bad weather rolling in, I really hoped we could get the hut set up quickly as I did not want to get caught in this bad weather. We carried on walking and we thought we had found the perfect spot but Fred turned around after several minutes of wandering in a circle and said it was almost perfect. Suddenly a clap of thunder startled us all and the heavens opened. We all cast out our magic and a huge umbrella popped above us and shielded us from the rain. This was amazing who would have thought that I would be able to conjure up a protective umbrella from the rain. The wind rattled through the umbrella and at one point I thought it would take off, but our magic was strong enough to hold it down. The rain continued for thirty minutes and went away as quickly as it had arrived. Fred flicked his fist and the umbrella floated away, Fred kept the spell active just in case the rain made an appearance again.

Fred shouted out that he had found the perfect place for his hut, he took out the hut from his pocket and flung it up into the air. It began to spin rapidly and was doubling every second in front of my eyes. It reached its full size and dumped itself on the ground with a thump, the door swung open and the fire crackled to life. I could feel the heat emanating from the door, Flora dashed inside and we followed, Fred shouted after Flora 'Make yourself at home why don't you.'

It was so good to get into the warmth of the hut after all that rain, I couldn't wait to get a nice cup of tea down my neck. Flora started flying around the hut getting all the bits together for dinner. Fred asked Flora to stop flying around so quickly as he was getting a little nervous of the fairy. She flew over to Fred and sat on his shoulder. She lent into his ear and whispered something that made Fred laugh out loud.

I asked Fred what Flora had said and he told me that it didn't matter. He asked if I would like a biscuit with my tea and I told him no as I didn't want to ruin the feast that Flora was cooking up. My mind started to tick over and over as to what they had to keep a secret from me.

I looked around to find Flora and couldn't see her anywhere, I knew they were both up to something. I sipped at my tea and felt like something was about to happen, I looked over to Fred and he started to laugh out loud uncontrollably. Fred fell to the floor gasping for breath between laughs, I knew that he couldn't stop. I started to panic and rushed over to Fred and called for Flora's help. I tried to calm Fred down but nothing would stop his laughter, Ned told me that I should do something quickly as Fred was in serious trouble. Suddenly a black shadow flooded the mirror, after a few seconds, she was here yet again, Lady Malaga spoke out from the mirror and said 'Looks like someone fell for my laughing curse of death, you are in a little bit of a dilemma.'

I shouted out to her 'Please help him, he isn't going to make it otherwise.'

She laughed her disgusting laugh and the mirror shattered with the octaves of her voice, the black shadow filled the room and suddenly she was in the room with us. 'I'm not all that bad Joe, If I help you now always remember I will want something in return. If you ever break our deal, I will make sure this curse comes back tenfold.'

I had no choice but to agree with her and she explained that she wanted the wand from Flora, I knew I couldn't touch the wand but Lady Malaga offered me a magical glove that would allow me to touch the wand. I agreed to the bargain but she warned that it would not change anything when we eventually came face to face. I knew this would cause disaster in the future but I had to save the life of one of my friends, I would face into my decisions in time.

Lady Malaga cast her magic inside the hut, this time it seemed different, the magic had a healing glow to its aura. The magic was white pebbled with gold flecks, it floated around Fred and pulled the dark magic that was infecting his soul. The magic poured out of Fred's mouth and filled the void above him, Lady Malaga flicked out a curse again, this time black magic, it destroyed the laughing curse of death in seconds. She turned her head towards me and said 'Remember our deal Joe.'

Her eyes flashed a vibrant shade of red and with a crack she disappeared. Fred clambered up off the floor, rubbing his throat. He asked what had happened and I told him. He was shell-shocked and didn't want to believe it. I thought that maybe it could have been Flora that had cast this curse as I did not see Lady Malaga anywhere near us when this happened.

I heard a sound towards the back of the hut, it was a voice and I ventured outside. As I did the voice got louder and louder, it sounded like to was coming from one of the trees. I walked up to the tree and noticed that it had barely any leaves, then with a pop a glove appeared out of nowhere, I knew this was the glove that would enable me to snatch the wand from Flora.

I picked up the glove and there was a pair of eyes that looked straight through me. I couldn't stop staring at the eyes, suddenly the glove wrapped around my hand and wouldn't let go. Everything started to melt away and I was looking at another world. In front of me was a huge rock with flames erupting from the top, Lady Malaga's form flickered through the flames and she spoke out 'You're holding my glove that will soon hold my wand, don't let me down or you will know about it. Don't forget I hold all the cards.'

Before I could say anything in return she cast out towards me and a flash of lightning forced me from her world. I was back outside the hut and could see Flora dashing towards me. She was holding her wand as usual and it was burning so bright I wished that I had some sunglasses. I shouted at her to ask where she had been and she replied meekly that she had been busy and I knew she was hiding something from me. I suddenly dashed to hide the glove from her and I went beetroot red with embarrassment at the thought of being caught with something that could steal the one thing that Flora held dear. I looked down at my hand and noticed the glove had vanished completely.

Flora spoke out to me and said 'Joe why are you so red and what are you looking for?'

I had to make something up quickly so I wouldn't get caught out so I said I needed some fresh air, she shook her head and flew down towards the ground and demanded that I follow her and she wanted to show me something. I knew this was how we would get out of the ends of the earth.

I followed her a little further into the woods and she waved her wand, she let go of the wand and it was in the air spinning rapidly causing a stream of flashing light. It looked like it was creating a bridge in the air, steps started to appear from the ground up towards the bridge. Flora turned and spoke 'Joe I want you to step up onto the first step, if you've told me the truth then the steps will light up green and will allow you onto the bridge, if not they will turn blue and I will have no choice but to call the other fairies.'

I shook my head and stepped up onto the step, it immediately turned green. Lady Malaga's glove must be a powerful item to hoodwink the fairy magic. I made my way up onto the bridge and Flora joined me and said 'Hold tight Joe, things could get bumpy.'

I grabbed the side of the bridge as we began to fly through the air at speed, my cheeks started to flap in the wind with the sheer speed that we were going. I managed to scream over the wind to Flora 'What about Fred, we are leaving him behind?'

Flora explained that he would be fine and that he knew that we needed to make our escape. She also told me we would meet up with him in the near future but warned me of the impending battle.

Out of the blue, Ned woke up and asked why I wasn't saying anything about the glove. He kept going on and on about it. I was that annoyed I shouted out NO… Flora spun into the air and caused the bridge come to what I could only explain as an emergency stop. She asked what was going on with me as I was acting strange and if I didn't tell her straight away then she would get mad. 'It's fine Flora, Ned was tickling my feet and I shouted out no to make him stop.'

She hummed at me and waved her wand, Ned was snatched off my feet and was dangled off the edge of the bridge. Flora asked Ned if this was the truth and for a fraction of a second I thought he was going to give me up. He didn't and shouted at Flora that this was in fact the truth. She seemed happy with his answer and magicked him back to my feet. I thought that was a bit harsh of her as Ned was now shaking from fear. She laughed at his fear and said 'I wasn't going to hurt him, I just wanted him to tell me the truth.'

She told me to hold on tight again as this is where it would get bumpy. Flora spun her wand again and the bridge accelerated faster than anything I'd ever been on. We flew over the last of the land, and the expanse of the blue sea with odd bits of land jutting out from the water. I was a bit confused as the land seemed like the safer option to take but who was I to decide. Flora pointed out where we needed to head to and it was just water for as long as I could see. The water looked a deep blue which made me think of how deep it was, waves crashed against the edges of the small pieces of land causing bits of rock to fall into the depths.

I asked Flora, where we would be landing and she looked at me with the biggest grin on her face. I didn't like the look of it at all. She spun her wand again and the bridge we were on started to become smaller by the second. My heart started to beat faster by the minute at the fear of dropping into the water depths below. She told me that I would have to jump from the bridge and to not attempt to cast any magic as it would not work here. I wondered if this was another test to see if I would be worthy to leave this place, I didn't understand what Flora meant by this but I knew I was about to find out.

We flew past some more dry land and I felt the time to jump was coming up, I looked at Flora and said 'I want to jump now Flora.'

She replied 'Go Joe, jump now.'

I jumped from the bridge and I must have misjudged my timing, I plunged towards the earth and hit a rock. The force winded me and I curled up in a bid to refill my lungs with the air I desperately needed. I took a gulp of air and everything went black.

I opened my eyes and a bight light was hovering over me, I could see Flora's wand spinning through the air but no Flora. I didn't have much time to think about anything, I jumped up to grab the wand and as I did the glove appeared on my hand. I landed back down onto the ground and couldn't believe my eyes when I looked and saw the wand between my fingers. Power tore through my body as the wand established its new owner, I felt unstoppable and then remembered Flora's words of warning that my magic would not work here. I looked around for Flora and could not see her anywhere. The only thought that was going through my mind at the moment was that Flora would be so mad when she found out that I had taken her wand. Would the other fairies come after me or did they have other powers without their wands.

How was I going to escape from this place now without the aid of Flora? Ned spoke out in my head yet again and echoed the warning that I was in so much trouble and that the other fairies would be coming after us, if they didn't hear from Flora.

I heard a cackle in the distance and the water at the edge of the rock started to ripple. Suddenly Lady Malaga's face reflected back at me from within the water. She spoke out 'Haha you fool, you have done exactly as I asked, it has come at a price though, look up there and see your poor dear Flora.'

I looked up and there she was floating in the air not even twitching a muscle. I shouted out to Lady Malaga 'What have you done to her?'

She spoke out again 'Don't you use that tone with me Joe, give me my wand or she dies in front of you.'

I didn't know what to do and I started to shake uncontrollably. I could not let anything happen to Flora so I agreed with Lady Malaga. 'Good lad, now throw my wand into the water.'

With a snap of my wrist I threw the wand to the depths of the sea below, suddenly Lady Malaga's body erupted from the waves holding the wand in her hand, looking more gleeful than I had ever seen her. She shouted out 'You really are a stupid fool, look again.'

I looked back up to Flora and she was nowhere to be seen, she had tricked me yet again. I heard her cackle and she said 'Here's your precious little fairy.'

A cage appeared midair with Flora trapped inside, the bars of the cage flickered with green magic keeping its prisoner at bay. 'Well I would love to stay and chat but I've got things to do. Joe don't be long, I'll be waiting for you. Oh do you know if fairies can swim?' Her cackling invaded my ear drums.

Lady Malaga flicked the wand towards the cage and it plummeted to the water. She turned to look at me and said 'Your choice Joe, face me or save your precious little winged creature.'

She waved the wand again and disappeared, her cruel laughter held on the clouds echoing all around us caused the water to foam and the waves to crash against the rock I stood on.

Chapter 8

SAVING FLORA

The waves forced the cage deeper into the water, I knew I needed to be quick if I was going to save Flora. I dived into the water and flipped myself as deep as I could under the water. I could see the cage falling through the murky water and I began to lose hope that I would be able to reach the cage in time. I forced my body and mind to edge deeper into the water, as my lungs started to burn and my vision started to haze there was a sudden burst of bright light surrounding the cage. It was so bright I had to shield my eyes even though the water dimmed a slight amount of the shine. Movement distracted my gaze, it happened so fast and then suddenly started to slow down like a film playing out in front of my very eyes. Realisation dawned and it was Flora swimming towards me, she grabbed a hold of me and then the next thing I knew we were both coughing and spluttering, floating on the top of the water.

Flora was fantastic, I was meant to save her but she had managed to save the both of us. Her wings started to flap and she lifted us both to shore, she turned and look at me with disappointment written all over her face. Ned started to laugh at me and I readied myself for the telling off of the century.

'Well Joe, it was only a matter of time before you would snatch my wand from me, I have been watching you from the day we met and I knew you would not be able to resist. All of the fairies warned me ages ago that someone would steal my wand and that person turned out to be you.' Flora shouted.

My mouth dropped and before I could apologise, Flora started round two of my telling off. 'This is what's going to happen Joe, I do forgive you for what you have done and I understand that this was not your fault. I knew what was happening and I had to go along with it so you wouldn't come to any harm, believe it or not Joe, I like you.'

I could feel the heat running up my cheeks as embarrassment started to flood my whole body. 'Joe,' Flora shouted pulling me out of the daydream that I was in.

'You need to do exactly as I say Joe, Lady Malaga now has the most powerful wand and when she truly realises its power, there will be no stopping her. She will be back before we know it and we have to be ready for her.'

'What are we going to do?' I replied.

'Joe, we need to find the tunnel that will lead us to the last destination and we can finally get out of here, it won't be easy and I'm going to have to call the other fairies for help. Some say I have the gift of foresight and trust me when I say, I need to keep you safe.'

My heart dropped and I knew I needed to take what I was being told by Flora into account, it sounded like there was going to be a big battle coming up and I started to wonder if Lady Malaga would actually harm any of us. Flora cast out magic from her fingertips and her wings lit up like a Christmas tree, how was Flora using magic without her wand, my mind started to boggle. Suddenly her wings lifted off her body and flew into the air, I turned to Flora and asked 'Did that hurt Flora?'

She laughed and said 'Not at all Joe, I had to warn the fairies and this was the only way I could do it now.'

I could see this was a good idea but Flora would be weak without her wings and I knew I would have to protect her. Flora explained that her wings would find the other fairies within the next hour and they would all come to our aid. We still had to find this tunnel and we all knew that it was going to be difficult.

Flora shouted my name and pointed in the distance, the clouds started to turn a dark grey and I made out a dark figure in the background, I knew this was Lady Malaga. The air crackled with an electric current shooting through the clouds. She had mastered the wand, she pointed it to the air and cast out. Flora was pulled up off the ground and caught in the spell which made her edge closer to Lady Malaga. She cast towards Flora and four other fairies were pulled from her body. Lady Malaga again flipped the wand and all five fairies started to shuffle through the air just like a deck of cards. Lady Malaga started to cackle and shouted 'Good luck knowing who the real Flora is now.'

She pointed the wand towards me and all of the fairies were in front of me and all singing out that they were the real Flora. Lady Malaga floated higher in the air and cast out a black smoke which surrounded her and vanished, her voice left an evil message behind 'hahahaha not even the fairies will know who the real one is.'

The five fairies continued shouting out my name and I became more and more confused by the minute. How would I find out who the real Flora was, I felt my magic was too weak to help at the moment and I felt the sudden pang of a headache coming on. The fairies Flora called upon would soon be here and they would be able to tell the difference, Lady

Malaga loved playing mind games with us all. One of the fairies flew out of line and started to walk towards me, wings had suddenly magicked back onto the fairies. Was this the real Flora I started to ask inside my head. The shouting was starting to ring inside my head and the pressure in my ears was getting more intense, I suddenly fell to my knees and shut my eyes, the shouting stopped and I think I must have dozed off. I opened my eyes and the shouting resumed stronger than before, I slammed my eyes shut in the hope that it would drown out the shouting.

I stood up with my eyes shut and I had to use my inner sense to get through this nightmare, my eyes started to flicker and the noise started yet again. It was so painful I kept falling to my knees. Lady Malaga's magic was much more powerful now that she had the wand. I started to feel scared about what she was planning to do next.

I knew I had to use my magic so I could see where I was going, I looked into my mind's eye and started to put one foot in front of the other. I noticed that Ned was no longer talking to me anymore and knew that Lady Malaga must have banished use of magic in these parts. A path appeared in my mind leading up to a small hill, I carried on walking and noticed an old battered sign next to the path. Words appeared on the sign as I got closer they read Magic is forbidden. A scroll appeared in my hand and a golden mouth appeared through the page and said 'Never cast magic in this land or there will be consequences, any warlock that attempts to use magic will be faced by the three rules that have been written into place by the one and only Mr Land.'

The mouth on the scroll stopped speaking and it all disappeared into thin air. The ground beneath my feet started to shed and make an awful cracking noise. I looked down and thought I was seeing double as the ground cracked open and a huge golden mouth sunk into the crack started to speak 'You there, you have broken my forbidden law and now must face the three rules.'

I opened my eyes and the sound that had caused so much pain previously had stopped and all of the fairies turned to look at me, there was one single difference in all of the fairies and I shouted out whilst pointing to the fairy I thought was Flora 'Flora that's you, you are the real one.' With that all the other fairies disappeared and the real Flora smiled at me and said well done Joe, you finally overcame Lady Malaga's magic.

More cracking noises started and then a single flight of stairs appeared leading down deep into the mouth that had appeared in the crack. I knew that this was the path I would have to take, Flora flew over to me and said 'you managed to beat Lady Malaga's last spell Joe, you can do this again. Think of everything you've faced so far this will be a walk in the park.'

She was right, I had faced loads of different challenges in my short time of life, the days were getting stranger by the day. Everything I had faced and was going to face would shape the person and warlock I was becoming. Without warning a loud screeching sound came from within the mouth, the voice sounded so familiar, I managed to place the voice and thought that it was my good friend Lara's voice. Without a second thought I marched towards the mouth and took my first step down into the mouth, the more steps I took the louder Lara's voice became. The steps spiralled round and down into the darkness below and the only thing I was concentrating on was the voice that was at the bottom. I looked back up and saw Flora struggling to make her way down, an invisible shield was stopping her and I shouted up that I would come back for her.

I reached the bottom of the spiral staircase and stepped from the staircase, the stairs vanished and I thought that I would be stuck down here forever. The only light that lit the place was a dimly lit old light hanging off the wall. It was cold down there and not much air circulated the place. The light started to flicker and a voice spoke out from the darkness 'So you made it then, I'm sorry for tricking you with that voice but I had to make you come down here. I will not apologise for that, look in front of you and grab that lever.'

The flickering light burned brighter and was as bright as you would find in a normal living room lamp and I noticed the lever in front of me, I moved forward and grabbed it. The voice shouted out and said 'Well done boy.'

I pulled the lever and the whole room changed appearance from the dimly lit room into a studio. Suddenly in the corner there was a ball of smoke, it was rapidly changing shapes and became a person. 'So you are the person everyone is taking about.'

My mouth dropped open and I was gobsmacked. The person in front of me was wearing all black clothes with blue stones decorating the jacket and top hat. His skin was fair and his glasses were blue with gold specks and his shoes were shining gold. 'You cast magic and now must face my rules. Don't be fooled, I may look like something from a fairytale but I am more powerful than you can ever imagine. I love game shows and this is one of my own creation, get ready.'

He took a hold of his hat and shouted for me to hold on tight, the room started to shrink and we were all forced into his top hat. His hat was another part of this land and I was the guest star on his latest episode of this crazy game show. Three games stood between me and freedom. 'Here is your first game, it is called cage the beast.' He shouted out.

What did cage the beast mean and whatever it did, did not sound good at all. I stood there contemplating what all this meant and Mr Land did a twirl and we were whisked away to another landscape. Mr Land was nowhere to be seen and the place I had been whisked to was dark and grey with a mountain range that jutted out from the horizon. Splitting the land was a lazy river running slowly towards its end. Then out of the blue, flying speakers appeared overhead and they crackled to life, filled with Mr Land's voice 'Now as you guessed from the name of the game, you have five minutes to cage the beast. A dragon is on its way to you and I've riled it up with a squirt of my magic potion.'

A dragon, you usually only see them on television and not in real life, what the hell was Mr Land thinking! Ned's voice spoke out in my head 'Yes Joe, a dragon, now get a move on and move faster.'

Mr Land's voice spoke out over the speakers again and said 'Good luck boy, I would be with you if I was brave enough but who would want to be in the same place as a dragon?'

I had to think quickly what I was going to do, this was a big scary dragon coming straight for me and I knew that it would most likely breathe fire. Everything around me was a big open space and I knew I had nowhere to hide, I started to run towards the mountains and saw a rock, I ducked behind the rock and realised it wasn't any good as my head was sticking out of the top and the dragon would see me. I really needed to think quickly and remembered this was a test and there must be a clue somewhere. Time was running out and I estimated that I would have around three minutes left to cage this beast. I heard a crash and on top of the mountain landed a large dragon which was red all over with yellow spikes, with an almighty spike for a tail. I shouted out for Ned to help and asked what I should do. 'Joe I have an idea, what you should do is face the dragon.'

'Face the dragon, are you mad?' I replied

'You have trained to be the most powerful warlock Joe.'

Ned had a point and I agreed with him that I would face the dragon. My hands and feet started to shake with nerves and I thought maybe this was not the best idea after all. The dragon lifted itself off the mountain and headed straight for me, the thought of being eaten alive passed through my head. My life flashed before my eyes and I spoke out inside my head, that it was nice knowing Ned. 'Joe get a grip of yourself, you can do this, don't just run away,' Ned shouted back at me.

The dragon was very close now and I could feel the wind created by its wings battering my body, it was bigger than any bus I had ever seen in the human world. This was it and I remembered this was just a test and that the dragon could not really hurt me. Suddenly a bright orange flame shot towards me, it was so hot it forced me to the ground I heard a massive bang and the ground trembled. I slowly pulled my hands away from my face where they had been protecting my eyes and the dragon was right in front of me staring. I managed to get my legs working, I pushed myself up to my feet and the dragon gave a massive groan, the breath that escaped from the dragon was so powerful it flung me up into the air, the dragon caught me in midair with its massive clawed talons. I felt like this was it and that I was done for. 'Why are you running from me?'

What the heck, did the dragon just speak to me and I knew the power of words had left my brain. The dragon lifted me up higher and opened its mouth and I could feel the heat of its fire coming from deep within. 'Well lad, have you got anything to say before you become my dinner?'

My heart stopped with fear and I started to panic that I would become the dragon's next snack. 'I'm sorry Mr Dragon, I know this is a test and I didn't see the point in running. I wanted to say hello even though I am terrified.'

'Say hello, a lot of people just turn against me and try to use their magic against me to try and hurt me. I have to defend myself and sometimes people get hurt which makes me sad.'

Wow the dragon must have a kind heart, it just goes to prove that you should never judge a book by its cover as the saying goes. 'I would never try to hurt you dragon, by the way do you have a name?' I asked.

'Yes I do, I'm known as Mr Scaly,' replied the dragon.

'It's nice to meet you Mr Scaly, do you mind putting me down please.'

'Sorry Joe, of course I can,' said Mr Scaly.

Mr Scaly, gently put me down on the ground and explained that I was the first person to be nice to him and in return that he would serve me forever. He told me that he would stay within my ring and if I ever needed him, that all I would need to do would be to call upon him. Wow, this was amazing, I now had a pet dragon and couldn't wait to tell everyone. Within seconds Mr Scaly vanished into the ring and the ring became burning hot on my finger and a yellow stone appeared. I still could not get over how magical this whole journey had been.

Ned spoke out in my head and said 'Well done Joe, I knew you could do it.'

A loud screech echoed across the land and demanded that we stop right where we were. 'How dare you take my dragon from me, who do you think you are?'

'I'm sorry, he wanted to come with me, I didn't make him disappear into my ring,' I replied

'Well, it must be true then, you are the most powerful I have come across, no one in seventy years has been able to do what you have accomplished,' Shouted the voice

I demanded to see who the voice belonged to and suddenly Mr Land appeared. He took off his hat and threw it towards us. It spun on its approach and from inside the hat scattered a sea of mirror sparkles. 'You have passed my games,' Mr Land said.

'I thought I had to do three games.' I shouted back at Mr Land.

'Well from what I have just witnessed, you don't need to pass anymore of the games. Please follow the path up to the hat and this will lead you back to Flora.'

The sparkles reached the floor and like Mr Land said a path appeared leading towards the hat. 'Thank you Mr Land and sorry for taking your dragon.'

'You are welcome Joe and you don't have to say sorry at all, the dragon has been waiting years to find a new master and I'm so pleased he has decided that it is you. Take care Joe and good luck with Lady Malaga.'

I took a few steps forward and stepped onto the sparkles, it pulled me up towards the hat and I got sucked inside the hat, it was the most beautiful thing I had ever seen, it was a kaleidoscope of colour with glittering pieces all around me. I was mesmerised by it all. Then it all suddenly stopped and it threw me out of a bright mirror and I was back on top of the ground where I had left Flora.

'Joe there you are,' Flora shouted.

'Flora, you wont believe what has happened.' I replied.

'There isn't any time Joe, Lady Malaga has captured all of the fairies!' Flora wept at me.

I shouted out in shock and complete anger, I had never felt anger towards another person like this before. Flora explained that while I was facing Mr Land's game that the fairies came to help Flora and Lady Malaga had turned up and captured all of the fairies and was too powerful to stop now that she had the wand.

I told Flora not to worry and that I would get them back, Flora was crying and tears ran down her face. She told me that Lady Malaga had left me a departing gift and handed me over a scroll. I ripped through the wax seal and unfurled the scroll.

Dear Joe

I admire what you have done and what you have been going through. There is only one way this will end and you know what that is. Don't be a fool Joe, I have taken the fairies and will dispose of them if you carry on with your foolish mission. I will give you one chance to save them and everyone else. Do as I say and everything will be ok. You know my story and you know I am not all that bad but don't push me Joe. I have left a map inside this scroll for you, use your magic and come and see me. I will see you very soon.

Malaga

'What does it say Joe?' Asked Flora.

Flora was so impatient that she snatched the scroll from my hand. I shouted at her to give it back. She shouted back at me that she would not give it back and I pleaded with her as it was important. 'Catch me if you really want it Joe.'

She started to run and forgot that her wings had been magicked back, she turned and looked at me and apologised and handed me back the scroll. I was sure she could be a Gemini as she had two personalities at times. I looked back at the scroll and noticed that the edge had a fold in it. I unfolded the scroll and found the map that had been mentioned in the letter. It pointed me towards a place called the sea of death and I knew that would be the way out of the ends of the earth.

Chapter 9

THE SEA OF DEATH

The scroll blew from my hands and dropped to the floor, the magic that held the map on the scroll disappeared and the map etched itself into the ground at my feet. I looked down in wonder and the map was pointing towards a tree in the distance, as we began our trek towards the tree, it lit up with brightness similar to that of a Christmas tree. We reached the tree and a door appeared built into its trunk, its carving was exquisite and this door shimmered with magic. The door swung inwards and opened to a path previously inaccessible, it led to a path down onto a beach that had sand stretching for as far as the eye could see, nestled against the shore was a small boat bobbing in time with the waves crashing against the sand.

The boat was tied to a huge rock with a rope that was golden and twinkling against the shimmer of the sea, I have never seen anything like this before. Flora bounced with excitement and flew towards the boat, I shouted at her to stop but nothing could stand in the way of Flora and her excitement. With an almighty crack Flora was forced up into the air along with streams of sand. A cage magically formed around Flora and I thought to myself what was it with cages always finding a way to capture Flora. 'Joe what's happening to me?' Shouted Flora.

'I told you to wait didn't I, but did you listen, no you never do,' I replied.

'Yes, Yes, Joe, you're always right, now get me out of here.'

The cage was floating high up in the air and I thought to myself, how would I save her this time. Mr Land's words of warning surrounding the use of magic still rolling around inside of my head. Ned spoke out inside my head and told me that I could use magic here and it would be fine. I panicked at Ned's advice but there would only be one way to find out. I cast out turning my magic through my ring and sent a spell flying towards the cage. The cage burst into tiny pieces as my spell hit it, the force of my magic sent Flora tumbling through the air and I sent another spell towards her, this helped guide Flora back to safety. Once Flora gained her composure she looked at me and I could see anger written all over her face, I told her that she needed to start to listen to people's warnings and not to rush in front of everyone else.

Maybe I should not have said anything, her face contorted with anger and her cheeks flushed with red, it was so red that I thought her head would explode at any minute. Ned told me not to wind her up as we all knew what she was like when she got angry. She flew off from us and I could see the sand start to shift yet again, I shouted out 'Flora wait, it's happening again.'

Flora turned around just in time as the sand shot towards her, her face got even redder than before and she started to scream and flung her arms above her head, the sand dropped back to the beach and lay silent once more. 'Wait… How did you do that?' I asked Flora.

She smirked at me but said nothing, I began to question how she had magic without her wand. This had to be impossible didn't it. She waved her arms again something hummed on the air, magic echoed across the clouds and darted towards Flora's body. As her power returned, the sand started to shift and the boat shot up into the air, the only thing keeping it from getting destroyed was the golden rope. I saw Flora raise her arms again, I had to do something to stop her, I cast out towards her and my spell knocked her to the ground. The sand once again settled and the boat floated magically back to the ground. I was relieved that my spell had worked and knew we had to do something about Flora, bad things start to happen when she loses control and we could not risk this happening time and time again.

I walked over to Flora and roared at her, why did you do that, do you care about anyone other than yourself?'

I sent a sleeping curse her way and she dropped to the ground with a massive yawn, I knew we would get out of this place safely now as Flora could not risk our mission. The thing with fairies was that they would lose control when they feel certain emotions, I called them anger fairies but would never utter those words to a fairy's face. I picked up Flora and carried her towards the boat. Once I safely put Flora into the boat, I cast towards the rope wrapped around the rock and it split and started to coil its way back towards the boat, I could feel the bob of the waves as we edged out to sea.

A wave caught the side of the boat and nearly knocked me on top of Flora, I moved her to safety and found an old blanket which I wrapped around her. The boat wasn't like any other boat I had seen before, from the outside it looked like a shabby old thing but once we were sat inside it, the floor materialised into a marble like substance and glistened in the sunlight. The sides of the boat were made from glass that gave us a view out into the sea that stretched for miles all around us, I could not wait to see what else I would discover.

I looked towards the front of the boat and saw two huge boxes, beside the boxes was an old looking door that had weathered over years. I walked over to the door and looked back over my shoulder to check on Flora, the blanket moved slightly with her breaths as she slept on. I began to open the door and the creak was loud enough to cause Flora to stir. I once again checked on her and saw that she had settled and was still fast asleep. Ned started to laugh at me and said 'This is really exciting Joe, it is like we are going on a ghost tour of this boat.'

I looked down at him and said 'A ghost tour of this boat, what do you mean... have you been here before?'

As the words escaped my lips, something flew from the door, it was so quick I could not see what it was or where it had gone, it was nowhere to be seen. 'Come on Joe, get walking will you, let us forget about whatever that was,' Ned said.

I could not just do nothing about what had flown out of the door and told Ned that I was not going through the door until I had found what had flown past me. I looked around me to figure out what the thing could have been and where it went. Ned huffed and puffed at me and he wasn't impressed as he wanted to go exploring through the door. I walked back towards Flora to see if the thing was lingering but I had no luck. I noticed a slight movement behind some more boxes on the other side of the boat. I yelled out 'There you are, come out I won't hurt you.'

A box was flung into the air like it weighed nothing and came hurtling towards me, Flora shouted out 'Look out Joe.'

How the hell had she woken up and got herself free of the blanket I had wrapped around her. I cast out towards the box and could feel some unearthly magic fight against my spell. I suddenly felt a break in the magic that had hurtled the box towards me and I took the opportunity to push more of my magic towards the box. I pulled the box back towards the ground and landed it safely in one piece. The shadow decided that it was time to move and jumped overboard and disappeared into the sea. 'What was that?' I asked.

'They call themselves the shadows of death,' Flora said.

'The shadows of what?' I yelled

'Death Joe, you know what death is,' Ned shouted out.

'Can one of you tell me what they are and where they have gone now,' I shouted.

'Oh Joe, you still have so much to learn of this world, they call them the shadows of death, they used to be humans but a dark force overtook their souls and forced them to take existence as a shadow.' Flora explained.

I told Flora that we had to find it and she laughed and replied 'Find it, haha, don't make me laugh Joe, it will always find you before you find it. Remember Lady Malaga wants to control all of the dark forces in these lands and will stop at nothing now she has the wand.'

'We have to do something Flora, this thing could cause us some serious consequences for everyone in this world and we have to stop Lady Malaga before she also finds the shadows of death.'

'Do you think the shadows of death were here by chance Joe, Lady Malaga makes things happen especially since she has got my wand... We don't stand a chance now,' Flora replied.

Flora was right but I couldn't just give in, we needed to have hope. Hope after all was the most powerful magic of all. There had to be something I could do to stop all of this. Lady Malaga knew that I was on my way and knew that I had to leave this place but she certainly was keeping me on my toes. This was all a game to her and the ultimate price at the end of it was her getting my memories of the past.

I told Flora to get a move on and to follow me through the door, Ned was positively gleeful but Flora on the other hand was huffing and crossed her arms over her chest in a mood. I needed to keep an eye on her or else my sleeping curse would need to come back out.

As we reached the door, Flora exclaimed 'Joe it is so pretty, look at that light.'

There was a beaming light coming from inside the doorway, it was a purple beam, with a hint of yellow and red dusting the rays. I heard Flora tell us to go through the door, she went first and as she crossed the threshold, she disappeared. It was almost like she had been teleported through the door. I took a few tentative steps towards the light and I was pulled into the light. It was like I was floating through the light. It felt amazing as the colours started to whirl and spin in front of me. I could hear Flora in the background shouting wheeee like she was enjoying the ride. Suddenly everything went still and it was as if my stomach was in my mouth, just like when you go over a speed bump fast in a car. I dropped for what felt like minutes and watched as I fell past a yellow dome onto a huge yellow slide, I hit the bottom of the slide with a Big Bang. 'Well that was fun,' Flora shouted out.

'I was not expecting that at all Flora, were you?'

Flora laughed and said 'Expect anything Joe, we are in a magical land after all.'

I knew that Flora was right and that I could write a book of all the adventures I had had so far. I wondered where the door had taken us, and if we were still on the boat at all. Flora turned to me and said 'You know we aren't on the boat anymore Joe, I've heard whispers about this place. The boat is just a little distraction and the door only opens for the most powerful warlocks.'

'Wow Flora, that's incredible, I did think that when we were on the slide,' I replied.

I began to wonder what I had to do now, I knew I wanted to get out of this place and face Lady Malaga once and for all. I missed my family so much and my heart began to ache with the memories of them. Once I stopped the evil Lady Malaga and saved the world from her, I could be the old me again and live my life in peace. 'Do you really think you could be the old you ever again Joe, don't be silly, you have changed the course of your future forever,' Ned said.

I kept forgetting that Ned could read my thoughts which in turn had helped Flora do the same. 'Ok let us not get anything confused, I know I am the warlock that everyone needs me to be, I just want to be back with my family and enjoying the comforts of home.' I said with a grin on my face.

'I wouldn't go that far Joe, you were the only person who let the most evil person in the world get access to the most powerful wand.' Flora said, crossing her arms over her chest.

'What is this both of you, is it pick on Joe time… come on we need to work together, I can't even work out where we are,' I shouted at them both.

'We're at the bottom of the sea Joe, look up and pay attention for once,' Flora replied.

I tilted my head upwards and discovered Flora was correct, there had to be gallons upon gallons of water above us. The only thing that kept it from crashing into this room was a sheet of glass. I looked in front and noticed an opening with a pathway that was lit with braziers on the walls, the light bouncing off several postboxes that littered the pathway. I walked over to one and there was a letter attached to the outer wall of the postbox with a list of instructions.

Upon the letterboxes you will find a series of questions, answer them correctly and you will gain safe passage, if not you will face the sea of death.

'Don't you get it Joe? You have to guess the correct answer at each of the letterboxes, if not the hatches on the glass above will open and the sea of death will flood this chamber and claim our lives,' Flora said.

Flora was right and the pressure she had applied to this situation was almost unbearable. I could not be responsible for the death of my friends.

'Right. Come on Joe, let us get this test started, and make sure we get this right, I don't want to be the sea of death's next meal,' Flora said.

'Just give me a break please Flora, the pressure is enough as it is. I knew I cast a spell at you and I'm sorry for that but you need to learn to control your temper at times,' I shouted at her.

Flora looked at me and if looks could kill, I would have died on the spot. She smiled at me and I secretly think she likes that I stand up for myself. I think she thinks she wants to get me ready for the tough decisions I will face in the not too distant future.

Right here goes nothing, I unblocked the first postbox and it sprung to life. The postbox split in half and each side was peppered with a different colour. One side red and the other green. In front of me a red and green card popped into existence. I heard a distant clicking sound and looked up to see what the source of the noise was, the latch on the glass above was loosening, I suddenly knew that I would have time to answer all the questions correctly. An almighty crash echoes through the passageway and I noticed the door had sealed itself shut. A disembodied voice spoke out and said 'A scroll with a question will shortly appear and you must answer it correctly, match the card with the correct answer and place the card on the correctly coloured side and you will pass this test. Fail and the sea of death will claim you forever.'

A scroll appeared and it looked like any touch would cause it to disintegrate, the golden colour made reading the question rather easy.

Question One

What came first, the chicken or the egg?

Flora began to jump up and down shouting out that she knew the answer. I told her to calm down and give me time to think, she tried to argue with me but with a stern look she calmed down. After a minute I asked Flora what she thought the answer was and she replied 'Well it was the egg Joe, think about it.'

Ned started to laugh and yelled out 'Don't be stupid it was the chicken.'

They both started to squabble and I couldn't concentrate to get the answer correctly. I had to shout at them both to be quiet. Their faces were a picture at being told off. I did chuckle a little bit and the pressure of our situation came back tenfold, we had to get these questions right. I shouted at them both 'This isn't a laughing matter, this could be the last place we are alive, if we are not careful, I don't mean to be harsh but we need to be careful.'

Flora stomped out and I was sure Ned tried to unlatch himself from me but my power was too great for him, he was no match for me now that I had gained much more experience. In his anger he squeezed my feet so hard I let out a little yelp. He soon gave up, he wanted to make sure I knew that he was annoyed with me.

I heard a high pitched whistle as pressure started to push its way through the hatches with the impending water. I had to be quick with my decision if I was going to stop this water from entering the chamber. I grabbed the card in front of me and noticed that it was the red one, on the reverse side the word egg was scratched into the card. I posted it through the red postbox as quickly as I could muster. The postbox lit up like a disco ball, whatever was happening had caught Flora's attention and she made her way back over to us. She spoke out and said 'Wow Joe, that's so pretty.'

'Well it looks like you have chosen the correct answer Joe,' Ned said.

I replied 'I think I may have Ned.'

'Well let us not just stand here, let us get a move on,' Flora shouted at me and Ned.

I really think she has a fairy anger problem. I said to Ned inside my head and looked down to Ned and could see his eyes become glazed with tears that had sprung from his intense laughter.

I told Ned that we needed to compose ourselves so we could get out of here. I had a feeling in my stomach that something bad would happen. We moved up to the next postbox, it looked the same as the last one but something was off. Within seconds the postbox leapt off the floor ripping a huge hole in its wake. Suddenly it sprung arms and legs and doubled in size. It kept growing and at one point I thought it would smash through the glass ceiling and bring down the sea of death on top of us. Flora took it upon herself to sort this problem and flew towards the postbox. As she did a huge gust of wind caught her unaware, making her spin through the air back towards us, all I could make out were her wings flickering to try and correct her balance. The wind stopped and Flora started to fall, I ran over and caught her in my arms, she was not having the best time at all. A voice boomed out 'Who goes there?'

I looked at the postbox as this seemed to be where the voice came from, 'It's me Joe.'

'Who is Joe and what are you doing here?' The voice replied.

'Joe Stone, why are you so big and what is your purpose here?'

'You what…. How dare you insult me with asking my purpose here, who do you think you are?' The voice replied.

I began to say I did not mean any offence when the postbox shrunk back to its original size and started to wave its arms about. 'I have never come across anybody who would answer me back when I was so big and scary, I take my hat off to your bravery.'

'I didn't mean any harm by it, what is your name by the way.' I asked.

'My name is Pat and don't even think to joke about the famous postman in the human world, that joke is far too boring now,' the postbox replied.

'I wasn't going to, I don't like being mean and joking about people's names, that isn't my style, nice to meet you Pat,' I said.

'Tell me what you are doing down here, we all need to get out of here, it is far too dangerous to be down here. I have spent years and years down here and now is our time to go,' Pat said loudly.

'I'm here with my best friends Flora and Ned, Flora was the fairy you spun around when she charged at you and Ned is my trusty boots.

'Sorry about that, I do seem to come across a bit touchy at times especially with my wind. It just happens when I yawn. I was placed here to warn others off and was cursed with the ability to get bigger. So when I yawn it comes across as a huge gust of wind,' Pat exclaimed.

He asked about Ned and looked down at my boots, I explained to Pat about the curse Lady Malaga had put on Ned and his sister in the dark gardens and Pat shouted out 'Never use that name here, it sends shivers down my post spine.'

I tried not to laugh but that was a good one calling it a post spine. Pat spoke out again and said 'Well it has been lovely talking to you Joe, but you best be on your way, I can see a bright man with a good head on your shoulders. My gift to you all will be to make the other postboxes vanish and grant you free passage from this place. You need to go through the green door at the end of this passageway.'

'Thank you so much Pat, are you not coming with us?' I asked.

'You're very welcome Joe, unfortunately I cannot come with you until the curse has been lifted. That old evil witch has a lot to answer for. Make her pay Joe for the greatness of us all.'

'That's not fair Pat, I promise that I will sort this all out and come back for you, I am on a mission to rid this world of her wickedness once and for all.'

'That's very kind of you Joe, but until she is gone for good, that won't happen. I wish you the very best of luck on your mission, please don't give me false hope. Now get yourselves out of here.'

It seemed like Pat was angry at me but I was only trying to help and not give out false hope at all. I made a mental note to come back for Pat and get him from this wretched place. I walked over to Flora and picked her up and walked towards the green door. I walked past Pat and didn't look at him as I could not stand the look of sadness in his eyes, he didn't even move an inch or look at me, so I continued walking towards the door.

Chapter 10

LEAVING THE ENDS OF THE EARTH

I walked through the door with Flora in my arms and a bright light lit up in front of me. I carried on walking and the feeling of familiarity washed over my body. In front of me was a path filled with lanterns, I looked all around me and noticed that I was back where I started, the feeling of elation washed over me as I knew what lay ahead of me. This was where I called home, the people I called family were just up ahead. I raced down the path with Flora flying beside me. On the horizon I noticed the hut with everyone poking their heads out of the windows looking at us. I could hear them all shouting my name.

I couldn't believe it, I came back in a big circle, I had faced everything that had been thrown at me and come right back to the beginning where it all started. I had missed everyone so much and couldn't wait to introduce everyone to Flora and maybe with the combined strength of us all, we could find a way to save everyone from the dreaded Lady Malaga. As I continued to run, I was looking everywhere for Blue but could see no signs of him anywhere. Alarm bells started to ring in my head, as I reached the end of the path, Sophie ran outside and shouted 'Joe, we have all missed you.'

'Sophie, it's so good to see you,' I shouted back.

We caught up with each other and wrapped our arms around each other in a massive hug. 'Where have you been Joe, we haven't seen you in years,' Sophie said.

'Years.' I replied.

'Yes Joe, you've been gone for two years.'

My heart sank at that news, how could I have been gone for two years, if had felt like a week at most. Time obviously moved a lot quicker in the lands I had been in. I didn't know what to say or think and said to Sophie 'I don't know what to say Sophie.'

'I do,' shouted out a voice.

I looked behind Sophie and couldn't believe who I was looking at, it was Dev. He shouted over to me 'So you think you can walk back here and think it is ok Joe, well it is not.'

'Dev…. What, how and where?' I replied

'Enough of your idle words Joe, you are no longer welcome here, in fact I've had enough of you already, you can go,' Dev sneered at me angrily.

Sophie shouted out at Dev for him to stop his nasty words and to leave me alone. He told her to be quiet and cast out with his ring raised in the air. A timer filled with sand materialised in thin air and imprisoned Sophie inside. Dev shouted out 'Look and learn Joe, this is what happens to people who think they can stand against me.'

The timer flipped itself over and the sand started to fall on top of Sophie. Dev started to laugh wickedly and shouted 'Say goodbye to your precious little Sophie.'

He cast out again and Blue appeared chained up, this looked like a shadow of the man I had left behind and I was powerless to stop Dev. Dev shouted out that he had been busy and that Lady Malaga would be so proud of him.

'Dev, stop this right now, I know you don't want to hurt anyone at all, I can see the goodness inside your soul, you just have to let it out,' I screamed.

'Silence, you will do as I say, by the looks of things you don't have much time left to save Sophie, she won't last much longer.'

'What do you want Dev, make this all stop please?' I replied.

'Well Joe, what I want is simple, I want that wand you gave to Lady Malaga. You will get it for me as I am the one destined to become the greatest warlock of all time.'

The wand, was he stupid enough to think he could go against Lady Malaga or did he have a death wish. I started to formulate a plan in my head and wondered if I could get Flora to get me one of the wands from her fairy friends. I agreed with Dev but said he needed to free Sophie first. He said no problem and waved his hands towards the timer. The timer smashed and Sophie dropped to the ground. 'No funny business Joe, I hold the ace card, let me down or your precious Blue will suffer.' With that Dev cast out and vanished.

I ran over to Sophie to make sure she was ok and she just looked at me but didn't say anything. Shock had overtaken her body with the possibility of nearly dying at Dev's hands. Since I had left this place he had become worse than ever before, he wanted to double cross Lady Malaga by trying to impress her and then taking the wand and making a stand against her. I began to question if Lady Malaga had done something to Dev during my absence and he wanted revenge. I knew I had to formulate a plan with Flora as I couldn't risk any more harm coming to Blue.

I needed to find more out about Dev and how he made it back, I thought Blue would have been able to deal with him but evidently not. It seemed like he had been holding people here as prisoners and that this place was not the same place I had left. Flora had taken a shine to Sophie and was flying alongside her towards the hut, I needed some alone time to come up with a plan so I walked slowly on my own towards the hut.

As I walked towards the hut to meet everyone, I noticed a strange glow in the distance. It caught my eye and I had a feeling that I needed to know what it was. It was to the left of the hut and it seemed like no one else had seen it or they were not paying any attention to this glowing light. I looked back to the hut and thought they all must have been gossiping about what Dev had just done. The light seemed to get brighter and a body-less voice spoke out 'Joe, over here I can show you the past and all of the things you have missed.'

I raced towards the light, as I got closer the light vanished and in its place stood a tall ancient mirror. This didn't look like a normal mirror, the glass was moving and looked like it was molten. I could just about see my reflection but it was all distorted, I got closer to the mirror and as I did, the water erupted from the mirror and latched itself to me. Before I could make a sound, the water travelled up my arm and onto my neck. I tried my best not to make a sound as I did not want to startle the others. I did my best to stop the water from travelling around my body but it was no good, the more I tried to pull it off me the more it spread. It overtook my whole body and pulled me into the mirror.

I couldn't do anything about it as I moved further away from the mirror it pulled at my body harder and faster. I attempted to shout out but no sound came from my mouth. I saw my legs get pulled off the ground and pulled into the mirror, I turned my body in an attempt to get someone from the hut to notice me, I saw someone running towards me but I could not work out who it was, it was too late anyway as my head was forced through the molten glass of the mirror. I looked back towards the mirror and could see the outside, Flora flew up to the mirror her little wings flapping wildly to keep her from being pulled into the mirror but it was no good, I looked up and saw that she was also a prisoner of the mirror.

Within seconds the floor under us disappeared and we plunged into darkness. How could this be happening again. I shouted out to Flora 'What's happening?'

'I don't know Joe, there has been echoes of this kind of magic before, this is what you would call dirty magic,' Flora replied.

'Dirty magic, what is that and how do we stop falling?' I asked '

Well I have seen this magic before, the pulling mirror is something of a legend in our fairy world. If this is what I think it is, the mirror is pulling us to a place where it wants us to be,' Flora explained.

'That isn't helping Flora, can't you do anything or have you got something you could use?'

We continued to fall and this was the worst feeling I had ever felt. I could only relate this to going over a speed bump too quickly or even bungee jumping both of which I was too afraid to try out. 'Joe it must be someone controlling the mirror, pulling us from the ends of the earth,' shouted Flora.

I asked if that could really happen and Flora explained that only very powerful warlocks could magic this kind of magic. All of a sudden Lady Malaga came into my mind and I reckoned that it was her doing this. She was the only one who was this strong and had the use of this strength of magic. We both suddenly dropped to the ground and a voice permeated the darkness 'Well, well, well, I didn't believe it would work, but it did.'

I looked around to gather my senses and to find out where the voice had come from, it was pitch black with very little light which caused further disorientation. I cast up several warlock lights and flung them into the air, light filled the space and dissolved the darkness of the place we had fallen into. I noticed a person in the distance and it started to turn around 'Surprise,' shouted the person and I knew the voice belonged to Dev before he had even turned around.

I tried to move but we were both frozen to the spot we had landed. Dev spoke out again and said 'You must think I am stupid, did you really think you could trick me…welcome to my world.'

Flora whispered 'Joe what have you done, what did you say to him to try and trick him.'

I replied ' I haven't said anything, not a word about trying to trick him?'

'Well he isn't very happy with you is he, you've managed to wrap me up in your meddling yet again. I planned on seeing the fairies and we both know this isn't going to happen is it?' Flora said as she folded her arms like she always did when she got annoyed.

Ned shouted to both of us 'Calm down you pair, arguing isn't going to help you is it.'

I explained to both Flora and Ned that the only thing I could think of that would have annoyed Dev was thinking of a plan to trick him in my own thoughts. I had never spoken a word of it out not even to my two best friends. Flora looked at me and shouted 'You idiot Joe, he can read thoughts as well, he clearly knew what you were planning and that's backfired hasn't it?'

I looked around and noticed that Dev had disappeared, a voice tickled its way into my ear and said 'Do you lot ever shut up, can you hear yourselves?'

I looked around to see where Dev was as I knew this was his voice but I couldn't see him anywhere. 'I'm right here in front of you Joe, open your eyes and look harder.'

Suddenly Dev was right in front of us and I knew he wasn't there moments ago. I shouted at Dev and said 'What has gotten into you?'

He smirked at me and said 'Just calm down will you, all that I did up there was for show. I called you into the mirror and this world to keep you safe. This is the only place that no one can watch us, this mirror is my own private world.'

I stared at him in total shock as confusion started to meddle with my brain. In utter disbelief I shouted at

Dev and said 'You could have killed Sophie, how do you think that has made her feel. Do you understand the importance of not scaring the life out of people? Do you really think I believe for a second that you now want to be friends after that little charade?'

'Don't you see Joe, I had to put on a little show to make it all seem real, if I didn't make it look real, I would have been done for.' Dev pleaded.

'You really are confusing me Dev, you have imprisoned Blue and I promise that if you have hurt him, the last thing you will worry about is Lady Malaga.'

'Relax will you, he is over there, hidden behind the glass in his own workshop working away. You can see him shortly. Like I just explained I had to do what I did to make it look real. This will get back to Lady Malaga and she will be pleased and she will suspect nothing,' Dev said.

Everything clicked into place and I finally got it, Blue and Dev were actually working together to fool Lady Malaga. Dev explained that they were working on a plan to get everyone out of the ends of the earth. He explained that he had to play the evil one to keep him on side with Lady Malaga. He knew that he would have to build a lot of bridges with people when this was all over but this was the price Blue and Dev had decided to pay.

I shouted over to Blue, that it was so good to see him but the glass shielded my voice and Blue remained focussed on the task he was working on. Dev moved forward and said 'You will have time to see him soon Joe, but you really need to play along with our plan. We will soon have enough magic to get us all out of here.'

I agreed to play along with this plan and hoped that it would work and that Lady Malaga could not sense the ultimate betrayal happening behind her back.

Chapter 11

PUTTING THE PLAN TOGETHER

'Will anyone suspect anything with me being pulled through the mirror?' I asked

'Not at all Joe, the mirror is the ultimate shadow screen. You appear to still be walking towards the hut and nobody will think anything different. We don't have much time to get you back up there, all you need to do is walk into your shadow and the swap will be complete,' Dev said.

Flora shouted 'Well let us get the show on the road, come on get a move on.'

Ned started to laugh at Flora's bossiness and Flora shot a dirty look towards him and said 'What's so funny Ned, spit it out.'

'Not now Flora, please let us get along, we will only succeed if we all work together,' Ned replied.

'Well whatever you were laughing at, I don't think it's particularly funny, you wouldn't be laughing if I had my wand,' Flora huffed.

'What do you mean Flora, are you threatening me?'
Ned said.

Flora laughed and said, 'Look who's laughing now,
I'm one of the best at changing the appearance of
shoes, I think you would look beautiful as a pair of
boots that are salmon coloured with yellow polka
dots.'

Ned gasped and said 'You wouldn't dare.'

I shouted at the both of them and said no she
wouldn't dare at all and told them both to hurry up
and get ready to leave. Dev told us to get ready and
for Ned and Flora to take their arguments elsewhere.
Dev cast out, power filling the space around us and
the ground started to move up away from the room
we were in. I shouted out to Dev and asked about
the plan, but before he could answer, the outline of
the mirror was in front of us. I looked out of the
mirror and was flabbergasted to see myself walking
towards the hut. I had to give it to Dev, he was
powerful and his magic was incredible to see.
Something dropped to the floor beside me and I
could see another scroll, I dreaded to think this was
another scroll from Lady Malaga with another map
on it, I hastily picked it up and unfurled the scroll.

Joe

You need to do everything that I tell you to do, this will be paramount in putting our plan together. Please act along with everything including if we have to battle against each other. Meet me at the lake's edge at 8pm and do not tell anyone about anything.

This scroll will disintegrate within five seconds.

I only just had time to read the scroll before the edges glowed with magic, and began to fall apart in my fingers. I stepped through the mirror and dashed towards my shadow. Just before the shadow of me reached the hut, I pulled it back inside me before anyone could notice anything unusual. Flora also did the same with her shadow, I looked in one of the windows of the hut and could see Sophie sat in the corner with shock still etched on her face. I knew deep in my heart Dev felt bad but I had to wait to see how their plan would unfold.

'Sophie.' I shouted, she looked up and stared at me and I saw a tear running down her cheek. I instantly felt bad for her and everything she had gone through.

Flora flew up to Sophie and perched on her shoulder. Flora's wings flew off her back and carried Sophie's tears away. I was in complete amazement that Flora would do this for someone she barely knew and I felt that Flora would help anyone with kindness in their soul. Flora looked at me and said

'Don't you worry Joe, I have relieved Sophie of this burden so she can rest and sleep well.'

I asked Flora where the tears would be sent and she told me they would be taken to the lake of tears. I looked on in shock and Flora asked if I had ever heard of the lake of tears and I shook my head. I asked Flora what this place was and she went into a full explanation 'The lake of tears is where any tears caught by fairy wings are taken, in the human world, tears just disappear but unbeknown to humans they are taken by fairies and fill the lake of tears, fairies are invisible to non magical people after all.'

That explained a lot and I remembered back to the days when I did not know magic existed in the world and would see people cry, I really thought that they would just fall to the ground but now I looked on in amazement at kindness of fairies. Taking people's tears and emotions away to help them feel better was the ultimate kindness. I was amazed that after all this time, I was still learning new things everyday and the old saying reverberated throughout my brain that everyday is a school day. Flora smiled at me and said 'That's the thing Joe, we all learn so much everyday, there has always been magic around us all but we all need to learn to open ourselves up to the possibility. Fairies will only let certain people see their wings.'

I looked over at Sophie and could see that she had started to relax and fall to sleep. I asked Flora 'Will you please take me to the lake of tears sometime please?'

'Yes of course Joe, when we have stopped Lady Malaga and saved everyone from the dark gardens and restored headquarters to its former glory.'

I knew that we had a battle on our hands and told Flora that we had best get some rest tonight ready for tomorrow, who knew what the new day would bring. I said goodnight to everyone in the hut as I also need to get some rest. I felt that we were so close to getting out of the ends of the earth. I looked around and noticed everyone had grabbed odd pillows and blankets and picked spots of the floor, it wasn't much but it would get everyone through the night. I grabbed a pillow and found myself a spot on the floor, I banged the pillow in an attempt to make it softer and shook out a blanket. I rolled over and noticed a bright glow and wondered if I would ever fall asleep. It was Flora and I only realised that when she started to rest, she would glow brightly. I asked her if I could cover her with a blanket so she was not like a bedside lamp but got no response, I guess she had fallen asleep. I suddenly remembered about the scroll and meeting Dev at 8pm, I stirred quietly as I did not want to wake anyone and I heard a whisper next to me 'Joe can you hear me.'

I jumped a little and wiped my eyes to rid them of the sleepiness, the person in front of me blurred into reality and I noticed that it was Blue. 'Blue.' I shouted out.

'Shhhhh be quiet or you will wake everyone, please follow me Joe.'

I got up from the floor and started to wake Flora as she loved coming with me wherever I went. I couldn't wake her up and Blue told me to leave her to rest. I didn't like the tone of Blue's voice and I began to think something was amiss. I began to doubt if this was truly Blue but I could not show that I was thinking this.

We walked through the hut and out through the main door in the place we used as a kitchen. As we got outside Blue's shadow started to get bigger and then the laughter started, in blind panic I raced back to the door of the hut but it slammed shut in my face.

'You foolish little man Joe, you're always falling for my little tricks. I have seen that you have been busy with your little escapades through mirrors and that you are cooking up plans.'

I turned back to the shadow and noticed that Blue was no longer there and that it was Lady Malaga. She reached into her dress and pulled out Flora's wand. She flicked the wand through the air and the magic that came out from the wand caused a huge draught all around me. 'You see Joe, this power is all mine and there is nothing you can do about it. You have been planning something with this little sleezeball haven't you? That will not do.'

She cast out her wand again and a cage appeared with Dev locked inside. 'Now we all know you've been a very bad boy haven't you Dev, thinking you could outdo me, no one ever has. Let me show you what happens to traitors.'

A spell hit the cage containing Dev and it shattered into millions of pieces. He was frozen in the air unable to move or speak. Lady Malaga flew up to where Dev was and touched the wand on his shoulder. A green light shot from the wand and worked its way down Dev's shoulder. She cackled and said 'This is what you call true power Joe.'

In a few seconds, Dev's body started to disappear into the green magic that was continually flowing from the wand. I shouted for her to stop but nothing would stop her cackling and her spell that would make Dev disappear for good. I could not let this happen and I knew I needed to do something. I cast out but my magic was blocked by the sheer power of Lady Malaga. 'How dare you try to disrupt me

Joe, don't think you can stop me.' Lady Malaga shouted out with her laughter.

She shifted her focus from Dev to me and threw her arm in a downward spiral, a stream of light erupted from the wand and smacked into the ground, the shaking made me fall to my knees. 'That was your warning Joe, you need to realise what really is real and not a figment of my imagination. I'll be waiting for you Joe, I am positively excited for our battle.' Lady Malaga shouted out.

Her dress glowed brightly and so did the ropes attached to her dress. She cracked the wand through the air again and disappeared leaving her laughter ringing through the air. The ground started to rumble and several snakes started popping out of the ground and slithering their way towards the hut. No one could enter or leave the hut without having to deal with the gift left behind by Lady Malaga. Flora was still inside the hut and I needed her help, I needed to get through the snakes to save her. I didn't believe Lady Malaga about Dev and truly thought she had captured him.

A snake struck out towards my face and I ducked out of the way just in time, I needed to distract them if I was ever going to get Flora to safety. The voice that belonged to Lady Malaga boomed through the air 'You think you can stop me, hahaha think again, be good little snakes and do your mother proud.'

I began to wonder what she meant by that, a single snake started wriggling its way towards her voice, it was like it knew something that I didn't, maybe it had a secret mission from Lady Malaga. All of the other snakes were stopping me from getting to the snake that was wriggling away from all of the others. I knew I needed some help but with Flora trapped in the hut I started to think. Suddenly a thought popped into my head, Mr Butterfly. Ned spoke out 'Thank you for thinking quickly this time Joe.'

'Alright Ned….. No need to be harsh,' I replied.

'Come on Joe, let us not argue, over the snake that was getting away.'

I called out for Mr Butterfly and I noticed him flutter against the horizon, he shouted out 'Hi Joe, long time no see, quickly jump on, where are we off to?'

I told Mr Butterfly to follow the snake and he flared his wings and we shot off after the snake. Mr Butterfly was having a hard time keeping up with the snake and gave an extra burst of speed to catch up. When we caught up with the snake, I shouted out for Mr Butterfly to watch as the snake reared its head to snap at us all. He didn't stand a chance as Mr Butterfly flew to the left and out of the way of the snake's vicious jaws. I noticed the snake carry on slithering along the ground. It dropped into a hole that had opened up on the ground.

Mr Butterfly dropped us next to the hole and shouted 'You'll be fine Joe, even you can fit down that hole.'

Ned started to laugh and I warned him that I was not in the mood for his banter. He apologised and said he wanted to lighten the mood. Mr Butterfly flew off and wished me luck. A small voice spoke in my ear and I dashed around looking for where it had come from. 'Who's that?' I shouted out.

'It is me Mr Wobble, down here.'

I looked down into the grass and couldn't see anything, I cast out and my vision multiplied and saw a worm slinking its way through the grass. He had a top hat and moustache with glasses perched on his worm nose. He explained that he had magic and would be able to transform me so I could fit down into the hole in which the snake disappeared. A mist that came from the worm started to envelope my legs travelling up my body and my vision started to get hazy.

I looked up and noticed that the strands of grass had become so tall they towered above me, Mr Wobble moved towards me and I cowered at his sheer size. He began to laugh and said 'There you are Joe, climb on, we don't have much time. I needed to shrink you so the snake would not see us coming. I've been so excited to meet you, everyone is talking about the warlock that will save us all. Mr Wobble shouted for me to hold on tight as things were about to get bumpy. He shot down the hole, and I instantly felt sick, I nearly fell off his back multiple times. Mr Wobble told me to watch myself as the tunnel we were in could collapse at any time, he was taking us a dangerous route as this was the only way we could catch up with the snake. I gave my thanks to Mr Wobble but asked him to make sure he would keep me safe. He told me that we were about to shoot out of the top of the ground and that the snake would be waiting for me. He told me not to panic and that the snake knew I would follow it. This was a test to make sure I would have the power to face the two trees.

We shot through a mound and the dazzling sun left me momentarily blind, Mr Wobble returned me to my original size. He bid me a fond farewell and said we would meet again once the witch had been defeated. I began to think in my mind that this snake was actually there to help me in an odd sense of the word and was not actually on Lady Malaga's side after all, but what was I to know. Mr Wobble disappeared in a puff of mist and I turned around to face the snake. I began walking towards the snake and it started to glow blue, the snake started to change shape. I noticed a blue hat appear first then a head and body covered with a long blue coat that flowed to the ground.

'Hello boy, I have been waiting for you, do you believe you have the power to cross the path of trees?'

'Hello Sir, I haven't a clue what is happening right now, you were a snake and now you are....' I replied.

'Silence, you are in my magical land now, I am Mr Howard but you can call me H.'

'I'm not sure what I have to do Mr H.' I replied.

'You call yourself a warlock, don't make me laugh, you're nothing here. You will be destroyed like the rest of them. You are no match for me.'

Mr H floated up into the ground and pointed menacingly at me and his hat flew off aiming straight at me. Mr H laughed his head off and said 'Keep still, it wont hurt me.'

'Joe, don't panic. I've got this,' a voice shouted out.

I couldn't believe it, Flora was flying towards me and kicked the hat so hard it flew back towards Mr H doing several somersaults in the process. I heard Mr H say 'No it can't be.'

'That's right H, you better believe it is me, and you've decided to pick on my good friend Joe,' Flora shouted.

Mr H floated back towards the ground and caught his hat and reattached it to his head. 'We're only messing around aren't we lad?'

I shrugged my shoulders and heard Flora shout out angrily 'You will leave Joe alone and will let him pass safely. If you don't you will have me to deal with.'

Mr H replied 'Of course, like I said we were only messing around.'

Mr H moved aside and Flora and I walked through two massive white trees that looked like they were covered in snow. 'Get ready Joe, this is where we leave the ends of the earth and head back to headquarters. Lady Malaga beware,' Flora laughed.

As soon as we passed the threshold of the trees, I felt myself floating in the air and then the whole space went white. 'That's it Joe, Close your eyes as things are about to get very bright,' Flora shouted.

I closed my eyes.

Chapter 12

THE HEADQUARTERS

I opened my eyes and memories came flooding back. I knew this room, this was my old room back when I was a student at headquarters. I began to wonder what was happening and why I was back in this place. I looked around for Flora and couldn't see her anywhere. I raced to the window and I could see the old training grounds, the window was filled with dirt and grime and I wondered who the warlock was that had occupied this room after me, they had not kept the room clean at all.

'All warlocks must report to the training ground immediately.' I nearly fell over with the fright that the voice had given me. I looked up at the wall and saw that there was a speaker on the wall and this was where the voice had come from.

'Well hang on a minute, I am not a speaker, I have a mouth and eyes,' the speaker said.

'I'm really sorry, you just gave me a scare.' I replied.

'Now listen and read my lips, all warlocks report to the training grounds immediately,' the speaker boomed again.

I couldn't get over how my old room had been upgraded with an angry intolerable speaker. I wondered what else had changed here but more importantly where was Lady Malaga. I made my way out of my old room and a shout from a voice I instantly recognised came from behind me. 'Joe, Joe, it's really you,' Lara shouted.

'Lara, it's so good to see you.' I replied.

'Joe, you won't believe it, Lady Malaga has the one true wand and she has also captured Dev,' Lara said.

'I knew she had something to do with Dev, do you know why we have been summoned to the training grounds?' I asked Lara.

'Your guess is as good as mine, the whisper out there is that there is going to be a battle,' Lara whispered.

I wondered why there was going to be a battle now and I began to think was this going to be the time that I had to face off against Lady Malaga. Lara told me that she had heard some of the other warlocks speaking about a battle in the lunch hall a few days back. A huge booming voice shouted out and said 'You both are to stop right where you are.'

Lara and I turned round just in time to see a spell heading straight for us. It wrapped itself around our shoulders and lifted us through the air. It felt like a pair of massive hands lifting us off the ground. 'Hahaha I've got you both now, you won't escape me again,' the voice spoke.

I asked Lara if she was ok and she told me that she was, the voice teased at us both again and I suddenly knew who that voice belonged to. It belonged to the guard from the prison from which I had escaped. 'Remember me do you... well this time there will be no escaping.' The manky old guard said.

Before I could do or say another word, the guard banged his staff on the ground and everything went black. I knew that we had been cast back into my old prison cell from which I had escaped all that time ago. The guard must have held a grudge for a long time to be waiting for my return. The stench filled my nose and I began to see around me, I was right, we were locked in that dirty prison cell. Rats ran their way along the floor and into cracks in the walls on the search for their next meal. It was a placed that filled nightmares. 'That's much better, I have you back where you belong, this time you have a little guest to keep you entertained. I'm going to have so much fun watching you rot here.' The guard sneered at us.

An almighty bang reverberated throughout the prison, along with a cracking noise that split the prison bars wide open. The guard looked confused and then dropped to the floor, his body causing the bars to rattle and bang. 'How dare you treat my guests this way, what makes you think you can get away with disobeying me.' The voice belonged to the one and only Lady Malaga.

'My Lady, I'm so sorry, I was going to bring them to the training grounds, I promise,' the guard replied.

Lady Malaga screamed in the guard's face 'Silence.'

I looked over to Lady Malaga and noted that she looked totally different. She normally wore a black dress decorated with lace and golden ropes entwined all the way around it. This time she was wearing a plain black dress with a shiny purple criss-cross pattern. Her hair was pulled up into a tight ponytail and her nails painted a metallic purple colour.

Lady Malaga's fingers crackled with a purple hue of magic and she aimed them at the guard, he was lifted up into the air and I could make out a faint apology. She brought her arms crashing back to hers sides and the guard fell to the floor lifeless. How had Lady Malaga just killed one of her own, I didn't think she was able to kill but here we were with a sea guard at our feet.

Lady Malaga looked straight over at us and we started to tremble with fear. My life flashed in front of my eyes. I looked over at Lara and could see the same fear in her eyes. 'Stand back both of you, this will not hurt in the slightest,' Lady Malaga said.

I closed my eyes and hoped for this to be over quickly and without any pain as promised by Lady Malaga. I suddenly felt a sharp piercing pain and felt myself fall backwards. I heard some shouting in the distance 'Wake up Joe.'

I opened my eyes and found myself back on the training grounds with all the other warlocks forming a circle around the centre. A voice boomed over the training ground 'If you have anything on you that you shouldn't discard it immediately.'

All manner of items were thrown up into the air, followed by a bombardment of spells that destroyed everything. A high pitched laugh sounded across the training ground and Lady Malaga appeared in the centre. Every warlock jumped back in fear of being caught doing something they shouldn't. 'You think it is ok to bring a stupid notebook onto my training ground do you?' Lady Malaga screamed whilst pointing to a girl at the end of the training ground.

'Come here now.'

The little girl started shuffling slowly towards Lady Malaga with tears dropping to the ground. 'Move it, I haven't got all day,' Lady Malaga shouted at the girl.

Lady Malaga wasn't very patient and she lifted herself off the ground and dropped down in front of the girl, they were so close I think I saw their noses touching. I heard Lady Malaga whisper to the girl 'Yes you're right to be scared.'

The girl replied, 'I'm really sorry Lady, I didn't mean to cause you any annoyance.'

Lady Malaga laughed her high pitched laugh and said 'It's Lady Malaga and it will do you well to remember that.'

She cast some green magic towards the girl and a cage snapped into existence imprisoning the girl until Lady Malaga decided what to do with her. Before anyone could do anything, the cage was cast away from the training ground and the sky lit up with the green hue from the cage.

Lady Malaga turned to the rest of us and said 'How rude that girl thinks she can interrupt me, who was she by the way. Someone tell me her name quickly.'

A tall gangly nerdy looking boy walked forward, his hair was slicked back and looked shiny. He stuck up his hand and Lady Malaga looked gleeful and said 'Yes what is it?'

'She's called Lisa, Lady Malaga,' He replied.

'Well Lisa has been taught a lesson hasn't she,' Lady Malaga said.

Someone shouted out in the crowd, what for having a notebook?' Lady Malaga's face transformed with rage and she shouted 'Who said that, who dares think they can speak back to me?'

No one came forward and everyone was standing still. Lady Malaga looked around the crowd and said 'Big mistake who ever spoke out, you will all suffer until someone owns up.'

She cast out a purple mist that touched everyone's heads one by one. When the mist touched my head it instantly gave me the worst headache I had ever felt. Dizziness took over along with a crushing pain which forced us all to the ground crying out in pain. We were like this for around ten minutes before someone shouted out 'Ok ok, it was me, I can't stand the pain anymore, please stop it.'

Instantly the pain stopped and the purple mist disappeared. I heard Lady Malaga shout 'Get here now boy.'

Someone next to me said this person was always causing the warlocks to be punished and they had all had enough of it. The boy stepped out of the line and dusted himself off. Lady Malaga grinned at him and said 'You stupid little boy, it is your turn to be punished.'

A laughter that made me feel sick echoed across the grounds and I looked behind Lady Malaga and saw Lara walking up towards her. 'Come my child, you can decide this little miscreant's punishment.'

Lara looked positively gleeful and said 'The stone curse for ten days.'

Lara cast out towards the boy and his feet started to turn to stone. She started to laugh and I began to wonder when Lara turned out so evil.

'Well done my child, you have grown into my perfect project, you have earned the right to stand beside me as I address this rat pack,' Lady Malaga said.

Rat pack! I'll give Lady Malaga rat back I thought. Lady Malaga started to speak again and all the other warlocks snapped their heads around to listen to her. 'After everything that had just happened unnecessarily, I need you to pay the closest attention. This is a matter of life or death!'

Life or death, what the hell was she muttering she continued her little speech and went on to say 'There is a war coming and I only have room for the strongest by my side. I need you all to focus on your training as I want you all to be ready for the War of the Warlocks.

I couldn't stand this any longer and shouted out towards Lady Malaga 'Oi that's enough everyone gets it, no need to terrify everyone.'

'Well Joe, I have all the power here, thank you for my beautiful wand. I forgot to tell you, the wand is now me, why would I need a flimsy bit of wood.' Lady Malaga raised her arms above her head and disappeared leaving the air echoing with her stinking laughter.

Lara stood and stared at me and then decided to walk off the training grounds. What had just happened and how would I defeat Lady Malaga now? Ned disturbed my thoughts and said 'can you hear yourself Joe, you're always whinging, just come up with a plan, you know you can.'

I agreed with Ned and headed back to my room to work out my plan. I needed this in place before the War of the Warlocks began to happen.

Chapter 13

THE BATTLE OF THE WARLOCKS

I entered my room and just like before the door slammed shut, the only difference this time was that there was no lock, the only way you could get out before was when the door was unlocked by magic. I began to wonder why this could be and Ned spoke out in my head 'I know why Joe.'

I asked him why and he replied 'Well Lady Malaga said there was a war coming, don't you think she's hoping for some of the warlock's to play dirty and come into other warlock's rooms to use magic against them.'

I agreed with Ned and told him, we would have to be on our guard at all times. I noticed the sun starting to set as it was casting its shadows over the bed, I knew that the light would soon fail and then darkness fall. I began to panic with the thought of being constantly on guard and that we could trust no one.

I lay on the bed and watched the door in case of any movements. I bolted upright with the sudden creaking noise that filled the room. I looked over to the door to check if someone was trying to get in but all was quiet at that end of the room. The noise got louder and louder and I jumped at the sudden voice 'Hey Joe, it really is you.'

It was the Silver Lion creeping from under the bed looking very smug with himself. 'Yes it is really me Joe, no need to panic.'

'Sorry Silver Lion, you gave me a scare, I thought someone was trying to get into my room.'

'No don't be silly, it is only me, one of your best pals from your time here before. You once thought of me as a monster under your bed but you know I'm friendly of course,' said Silver Lion.

'Yes Silver Lion, what can I do for you on this fine evening.' I said with a stern tone of voice.

'Joe, that isn't funny, your tone of voice was rude and unappreciated. You know that I won't bother with you,' Silver Lion shouted.

I shouted out for him to wait and I didn't mean to upset him but it was too late, he vanished back under the bed. I wondered what was wrong with him and Ned spoke out 'I'm not sure what's wrong with him, maybe you offended him. You should stop stressing out and don't take it out on the people and things who care about you.'

I understood what Ned was saying and decided that I needed to get some rest to stop being grumpy with everyone. Ned said he would keep a watch out and wake me up if anyone came through the door. I told Ned thank you and that I would see him when I woke up. Within minutes of my head touching the pillow, I was out for the count. I suddenly opened my eyes to someone shouting 'Morning, sleepy head.'

'Is it really morning, you should have woken me up Ned, I didn't mean to sleep through the night that's not very fair on you.' I spoke sleepily.

'It's ok Joe, you needed the rest and I can rest anytime, I am on your feet after all with you doing all the work.'

I laughed at Ned and agreed with him. I wondered what all the noise was and Ned told me that all the warlocks were fighting against each other and that only the strongest warlocks would survive. I knew we had to do something to stop this madness. I heard some commotion outside of the door and heard a warlock gossiping and they said that they were proud of themselves for creeping into a room last night and punishing him with magic. I heard another voice gasping and asking if they were ok. I didn't hear the response as they started to whisper to stop people eavesdropping on their conversations.

I didn't know how I would find out either, I could not be seen going behind Lady Malaga's back. I needed to keep her on my side for the time being as I needed to make sure I was ready for when the battle came. I spoke with Ned and we both agreed that we would stay on our toes but act coyly to try and find out what all the other warlocks were planning. I had a feeling that the ghost spell would come in handy during my stay at headquarters. I told Ned that we needed to get ready to see what the day would bring.

As I was getting ready I heard rustling under the bed and dashed to catch a look, thinking that it would be Silver Lion but it wasn't. Under the bed was a green shaped object and wondering what it was, I reached out to grab it and as I did a tiny green spike punctured my finger. I shouted out in pain as the spike embedded itself further into my flesh. I heard a little laugh and the object said 'that will teach you won't it, how dare you try to grab me.'

The object turned around and I looked upon a green ladylike object, perched on top of her head was a massive mop of pink hair and neon pink lipstick. I shouted out still in shock from being injured by something so small 'I'm sorry, I didn't realise you were under my bed, I don't even know you.'

'You don't know who I am, where have you been? Don't think you can mock me with your idiocy. My name is Spell Dander,' the green lady replied.

'Spell who.' I asked.

'You are skating on thin ice, how dare you mock me and don't think you can look down on me for one minute,' Spell Dander shouted.

Spell Dander shot out a spell from her fingertips and I was whisked away and perched on the edge of a mountain, a few inches from a perilous fifty foot drop. I hated heights and felt my heart begin to race and my hands become clammy. I heard someone shout out for Spell Dander to stop this and I was instantly transported back to my room. I heard laughter and looked around to Spell Dander and she said 'Oh hi Silver Lion, nice to see you after all this time, the boy mocked me so I needed to teach him a lesson.'

Spell Dander and Silver Lion started a deep conversation and I heard Silver Lion ask why she had come back and Spell Dander said that she had heard that Lady Malaga had gained possession of the most powerful wand and that she had to see it to believe it. I heard Silver Lion give Spell Dander a word of waning about being here again and that she shouldn't have come back especially with what happened last time. I shouted out 'What happened last time...tell me?'

'Do you want to shout any louder Joe?' Spell Dander said with aggression written all over her face. She looked that angry I swear I could see some of her pink hair fall out. Silver Lion interrupted and explained that would be a story for another time and that we had to get Spell Dander to safety. I offered my help and was laughed away and was told that I wouldn't be able to help as I wouldn't be able to find my way out of a magical bag. I began to wonder why Silver Lion and Spell Dander were so easily offended.

Spell Dander spotted Ned on my feet and said 'Well, well, well, Ned, still up to no good and finding other people to do your dirty work are you?'

I had had enough with Spell Dander, who did she think she was coming here giving us all this abuse, I shouted out to her 'Why don't you go and get found by Lady Malaga... you're not wanted here.'

'Take that back or both you and Ned will be sorry,' Spell Dander shouted.

I screamed back in her face and said 'Never, I meant it, just do one will you.'

Page 176

Spell Dander flung her fingers in the air and a spell crackled towards Ned, he transformed in front of my eyes and the laces which stood boring and dormant became a pair of fluffy pink laces with yellow spots all over.

'I'll get you back for this Spell Dander, just you wait.' Ned shouted at her.

'Hahaha, I'd like to see you try. Enjoy your new look for the next twenty four hours.' With a twist of her pink hair, Silver Lion and Spell Dander disappeared.

I looked down at Ned and tried to prise him off my feet, he would not budge. I shouted out to Ned and cursed him for taking the brunt of Spell Dander's curse. How would I face the other warlocks now without being a laughing stock. I had this for the next twenty four hours. I began to cast a transformation spell and Ned shouted 'It won't work, don't even attempt it.'

Ned looked up at me with very sad eyes and kept apologising. I told him it would be ok and that we would face anything that was to come together. I began to walk towards the door and make my way down to the training grounds. As I walked out into the courtyard, another warlock started to laugh and said to the other warlocks 'Hahahahaha lads come and look at this.'

I turned around and could see several other warlocks running towards me with the ringleader being a lad called Big Scott. He was the headquarter's bully and was notorious for taunting people. 'Look what we have here lads, pink fluffy shoelaces, we don't allow this in headquarters do we lads?'

I heard one of the other lads shouting out for them to grab us and Ned said 'Joe make a run for it, get ready as I'll use my extra running ability.'

'Ok, let me say something back before you do, I will not let them bully me the way they have bullied so many other people in the past.' I said.

'Yes that's right Scott, I do have pink fluffy laces and I love them, what about you though hey, you must be a lonely little person if you find pleasure in bullying other people,' I shouted back to Scott.

Scott's face was an absolute picture and I would say that it had tinged pinker than my new laces. I heard one of the other lads shouting that we were done for. Just in the nick of time Ned started to run and I felt the power flow through my feet. A punch came really close to hitting me square in the jaw and I made a mental note to thank Ned later.

Before I knew what was happening and where we were, I spotted the dreaded dark gardens in front of us. Ned kept running and running and I looked down and nearly tripped over. 'Ned I think we should stop now. Let us make our way back to our room. We can keep an eye out for Scott and his gang from there. This isn't the last we have heard of them.'

'Joe I think you are forgetting who you are, you are the most powerful warlock that has ever stepped foot in this headquarters. If you wanted to get back at Scott and his gang, use your magic and cast them from this place forever,' Ned spoke out as he slowed down.

'I know that Ned but I don't like to use my magic to its full potential just yet. I need to save my strength and magic for the battle against her. It's far more important to save the world and everyone in it than battle against a few bullies who haven't got anything better to do. I replied.

'Joe, I love that you respect every other warlock so much regardless of what they have done or plan to do. Why can't every warlock be like you?' Ned asked.

I began to contemplate what Ned said as we headed back to our room.

Chapter 14

LARA

'Lara what are you doing here?' I shouted out as I got back to my room.

Lara was waiting outside looking very shaken and scared. Her arms were pulled across her body like she was hugging herself. As soon as she saw me, she grabbed hold of my arm and pulled me into my room. 'Get in quick,' she shouted.

'Lara, quit pulling my arm and tell me what the heck is going on?' I said.

'Yeah Lara, what's with pulling people around like they are rag dolls,' Ned said in a animated voice trying to be funny.

'Joe, Ned, I have seen Lady Malaga's plans and they are frightful to say the least, you won't believe what she's planning,' Lara cried.

I asked Lara to tell me more and she went on to explain that there was going to be a huge battle ahead and that Lady Malaga planned to rid the world of all goodness. My heart dropped hearing the words coming from Lara's mouth, I began to wonder what a world would be like without goodness and light in it. I shuddered at the thought, Lara went on to explain that Lady Malaga wanted to steal all the other fairy wands and manipulate them with magic and give this power back to the warlocks once and for all. She would also use the fairies as the life blood for the wands to work.

I hugged Lara and told her that it would be ok, that I too also had a plan and wouldn't let this happen. 'Joe I don't have much time left, Lady Malaga knows I've been spying on her, but I felt you had a right to know what was happening. I'm sorry about that boy on the training grounds, but I had to act the convincing part in front of her.'

I reassured Lara that nothing would happen to her and that I would do my best to save her from harm, I was flabbergasted to find out that Lady Malaga wanted to use the fairies in such a heinous way. Lara told us that there would be a meeting later on the training grounds and all the warlocks would become a hunting party of sorts to round up the fairies that had escaped from Lady Malaga's clutches the first time around. It seemed like she wanted all the fairies dead for her most evil of acts to work. The wands were taken from the warlocks to save this world and now the plan was to give them back, I was sure disaster would follow on from her most dreadful plan.

'Joe, please do something, you can't let this happen,' cried Lara.

'It's ok Lara, I will do everything I can, I need some help finding other warlocks who want to make a stand against her,' I replied.

A strange hissing sound had us all looking around and we noticed green smoke start to pour from under the door. A sneering laughter filled the air and I knew this was going to be the end of our little meeting. Lara turned to me and said 'It's Lady Malaga Joe, I can't see anything, please help me.'

'Lara where are you, I can't see or hear you,' I shouted.

A foul and loathsome voice filled the air and said 'Stupid Joe, how dare you think you can ruin my greatest ever plan... you will never see your darling little Lara again. The next time you see her, she will be my greatest creation.'

I shouted out for Lady Malaga to leave Lara alone but her voice crackled through my room once more 'Silence... You will come to the training grounds with everyone else. Say goodbye to your little girlfriend Lara.'

The green smoke started to thin out of the room and I looked around, gone was the evil voice along with

Lara. I knew that I had to keep up this charade with Lady Malaga and made a move to head towards the training grounds. The speaker on my wall sprung to life and said 'All warlocks are to attend a mandatory meeting on the training grounds at 6pm. Lady Malaga has some important information she wishes to share.'

I paced in my room for a moment mentally preparing myself for whatever this news would be. I began to wonder what had happened to Lara and what did Lady Malaga mean when she said Lara would be her greatest creation. I climbed onto the bed wanting a lie down as I could feel a headache coming on from anxiety and stress. I heard a small voice across the room that said 'Come here Lady.'

I began to wonder who this could be and looked to the floor and saw that Silver Lion and Spell Dander were back. They were chasing each other around the room with Silver Lion trying to catch Spell Dander.

I shouted at them both to stop running and noticed that Spell Dander had donned a hat and sunglasses, I wondered why she would need sunglasses whilst she was indoors. 'It was only a joke, stop being stupid.' Silver Lion exclaimed.

'Why are you both chasing each other around, someone explain what is going on?' I shouted at them both.

'I changed Spell Dander's hair colour to blue as payback for what she did to Ned and now she thinks I am being evil chasing after her.'

At this I burst out laughing and said 'What's with the sunglasses though?'

Spell Dander shouted back 'He only went and changed my eyebrow colour as well…. It is not funny Joe.'

With this she cast out and I narrowly missed the spell she flung my way. I looked back at the wall where her spell had collided and saw that it had been a peppered blue. Spell dander wanted to give Joe a taste of the blue treatment she had been given but had missed. I demanded that Silver Lion apologised to Spell Dander and Ned spoke up suddenly and said 'don't worry about me anyone, just pretend I'm not here.'

'This is all your fault anyway Ned, so you can keep it shut,' Spell Dander shouted.

'My fault, can I remind you it was you who turned my laces pink, or did you forget about that,' Ned replied.

There was so much shouting back and forth between them and the argument got a little boring, I shouted out to the pair of them 'Will you stop bickering, there is far more important things at hand, think about everything else instead of yourselves for a change. Lara could be anywhere and the fairies face certain death if we don't do anything.'

Spell Dander's ears popped up at my warning and looked me dead in the eyes and said 'no one will hurt my friends and gets away with it.'

Silver Lion agreed and it seemed like everyone had made up and were friends again. I said to them to follow me and stop the evil Lady Malaga. Spell Dander spoke up and said 'Yes Joe, you can do it, kill her once and for all.'

'No, I'm the warlock that will not kill, there has to be some goodness left in her and I will find it in other ways, death is too final even for Lady Malaga.'

'No Joe, the goodness in the evil witch's heart died long ago, we need her killed this time to make sure she can never return,' Spell Dander said.

'No one is killing anyone, not whilst I still have breath in my lungs,' I shouted at Spell Dander.

I didn't think Spell Dander meant for me to kill her and was coming across harsh in front of everyone. I thought she meant to kill the evil in her soul and save her once and for all but who was I to know, it seems like Lady Malaga and Spell Dander had some history between them. I asked everyone if they knew of a spell that would help with this and Ned spoke up 'Joe I knew of a spell many years ago, I remember being taught something like this in a history lesson. You need to know the exact incantation but no one ever speaks this forbidden spell anymore.'

Something clicked in my head suddenly and I felt the making of a plan start to come together. I remembered that I had the knowledge to bring things back from the dead, what if I could master a spell that would sever the evilness from Lady Malaga's soul. 'Right you lot, you need to disappear and come back later on, I need to think about heading to the training grounds, please keep an eye on everything from your secret room you showed me many years ago.'

I bid them all goodbye and only kept my trusty friend Ned with me, I heard both Spell Dander and Silver Lion start to scuttle back under the bed, I quickly turned to them both and said 'You both never told me how you know each other.'

'Joe that is a very long story for another day, I could write a book with everything I could tell you,' Silver Lion chuckled as he made his retreat.

'When I next see you both, I expect you to have changed Spell Dander back to her original appearance Silver Lion, that's the way you can make it up to her,' I said to both of them but I heard nothing in response.

I walked over to the bookshelf in the corner and grabbed off the dustiest and heaviest book I could find. I wanted to distract myself with a good book whilst I made my way to the training ground. I left my room and heard a shout behind me 'Lady Malaga doesn't allow books on her training ground and you will be punished.'

It was one of the bullies from earlier on that belonged to Scott's crew that had said it and I looked behind me and smirked 'It's fine, I can make this book vanish before Lady Malaga even realises that I've got it.'

'Not before I'll tell Lady Malaga myself,' the bully shouted.

Joe knew that he could not take the risk with this bully, he cast a spell out which made the bully's arms and legs snap together and froze him to the spot. He pushed the bully back into his room and cast the vanishing spell, the bully vanished in the blink of an eye. I went back to flicking through the book and found exactly what I was looking for. The bounce back spell. I began to think that if I made this book vanish whilst on the training ground, then any magic that Lady Malaga cast would rebound and weaken her defences. This may give me a little bit of time to come up with phase two of my plan. I felt bad for casting my magic against another warlock but I knew that I could never risk the plan getting out. I walked over to the training grounds and noticed all of the other warlocks starting to assemble, the excited chatter amongst them bouncing around my ears. I looked over to where Lara would usually be and the space was empty, I hoped and prayed that she would be ok.

Suddenly the green smoke started to flood out from the middle of the training ground, I looked over towards one of the teachers and noticed that they had called one of the others over to them and started to whisper hurriedly. I started to wonder what they were saying, one of the teachers let out a piercing scream and they were lifted up into the air. The teacher began to cast out magic to try and stop whatever was causing the commotion. I did not recognise this teacher and thought that she must be new to the school.

A sickening voice filled the air and boomed 'It is terribly rude to talk when I am arriving, how do you plead?'

The teacher was floating in the air and before she could utter her reply, there was a flash of lightning and the teacher froze suspended in midair. The looks on everyone's faces were what you would usually find on a halloween evening. 'Catch.' Lady Malaga shouted.

With a flick of her wrist the teacher began to fall from the air, seconds before the teachers would have been broken into millions of pieces, another teacher jumped to the rescue and cast magic to save the other. I instantly recognised this teacher, it was Mr Fire. I heard him shout out 'I've got you, you're safe with me.'

The other teacher wasn't frozen permanently, as this was a spell for Lady Malaga's amusement. A tear fell down the teacher's face as this was the only thing that was not frozen. 'Anyone else want to talk, go ahead... it's you that will be sorry,' Lady Malaga shouted to the crowd.

I looked around the crowd of warlocks and noticed that they were very still, not even their lips were moving, the threat of being frozen still lingering over them. Lady Malaga went on with her speech 'I would like to introduce you to somebody, please meet the most famous fairy of them all.'

With that Lady Malaga twisted her body around and you could feel magic reverberate across the training grounds. A sudden popping sound caught my attention and there was my best friend Flora, twisting and floating through the air. She looked to be fast asleep but I knew what the sleeping curse truly looked like. 'You've killed her, how could you?' Shouted an unknown warlock.

'Silence, all of you pay attention, this is what is going to happen. I want you all to capture the fairies that have escaped my clutches. I want all of the wands and any of you that do not want to be a part of this will die here on these grounds. I want all of the power this world has to offer and you all will obey and in time so will the whole world.'

Everyone's mouths dropped open in horror and not another word was spoken. Some of the warlocks decided to cast themselves out from the training grounds and I assumed they were heading to the fairy lands. I looked over and noticed one young warlock girl was crying and saying that she couldn't harm another fairy. Lady Malaga noticed her and lifted the girl from the ground and pulled her towards the centre of the training grounds. Lady Malaga screamed in the girl's face and said 'what are you waiting for little girl, do as I demanded of you.'

The scared warlock could not move a muscle due to fear of what would happen and started to sob uncontrollably. She looked Lady Malaga in the eyes and screamed 'I will not hurt another fairy, you evil witch.'

Lady Malaga began to cast her magic at the warlock's feet and everyone watched as the girl's legs started to turn to ash, black, dark and dank just like the evil you would expect from Lady Malaga. Just as we all thought it was too late for the girl, Lady Malaga spoke out 'Have you a change of heart yet young one?'

No words came from the girl's mouth and we all realised that it was too late for her now, her body dropped from Lady Malaga's magic and was dumped to the floor. Ash in place of what was once a beautiful young warlock. Lady Malaga looked gleeful and turned to the warlock's who remained behind 'If any of you are having second thoughts and want to disobey me, you can join your little friend and become my newest creation... a garden of ash.'

Within seconds the remaining warlocks cast themselves to the fairy lands to do Lady Malaga's bidding. Lady Malaga seemed happy with herself and cast herself and Flora away from the training grounds. I really hoped that I wasn't too late to save one of my greatest friends. I knew that the time to stop this evilness had come and somehow Lady Malaga's reign of terror was going to come to end.

Chapter 15

THE CAPTURE

I cast myself out along with the other warlocks to the fairy lands, when I arrived it was like something had changed. The other warlocks were running around following Lady Malaga's orders scared to turned into ash if they didn't. It was like this had become the big hunt and no warlocks were showing any compassion. I looked over my immediate surroundings and one of the warlock's had cornered one of the fairies in the fairy garden and was taunting it. He cast out and a blue net surrounded the fairy and crackled with magic stopping the fairy from using her wand to escape. 'Got you…. Lady Malaga will be so pleased,' shouted the warlock.

Before I could do anything, the warlock grabbed the net and cast himself back to headquarters to hand over the fairy to Lady Malaga.. It had become a race for the warlocks, they wanted to see how many fairies they could catch each. I knew I had to play along and also capture a fairy, this would break my heart but I had to keep up my fake persona.

Word got around fairyland quickly that an ambush was in progress and that the fairies were being hunted down. Only a few of the warlocks had managed to snare a fairy and the heat was on me to get myself a fairy prisoner. I ran into the old tree trunk and dashed through the rooms, some of the other fairies were flying round flicking magic at the other warlocks. I cast out my magic and it hit a fairy's wings and she fell to the floor. I magicked up a bag and dropped the fairy inside, I sealed the bag with magic to make sure she could not escape and cast myself back to headquarters.

As I returned to headquarters Lady Malaga was ready and waiting and did not seem happy at all. It appeared only seven warlocks had managed to capture a fairy, Lady Malaga wanted a lot more. She locked the fairies in a cell and I could sense a shift in her panic as she knew the other fairies would come and attack her headquarters. Once the fairies banded together they would become a formidable force and Lady Malaga knew this. Lady Malaga assigned seven warlocks to watch over the fairies to make sure they could never escape.

She gathered everyone back on the training grounds, as she wanted to see who was worthy of holding a fairy wand. I couldn't believe what was happening right now and could no longer stand it, I cast out and could feel my magic powered by my rage and anger. My spell lifted the warlocks from the ground and surrounded them with a strange yellow glow. I had never seen anything like this before. Lady Malaga looked amazed and shouted across to me 'You sure have some power there Joe, you've done it again.'

'What do you mean, it was you who made me do this,' I replied.

'You've done exactly what I wanted you to do, thank you for granting me access to your memories, they have been hidden for such a long time.' Lady Malaga cackled.

Lady Malaga shot magic towards me and the yellow glow that had ensnared the warlocks seeped out of my soul and was pulled towards Lady Malaga. She shouted out to me 'Thank you Joe, I now have the magic to destroy your precious little world, thank you for remembering the spell. I knew the fairies would be the ones to lead me to it, you just needed a little push. As for those pesky little creatures, they're your problem now.'

It suddenly dawned on me, that I had given Lady Malaga the greatest weapon I ever could. She never wanted the fairies, it was all a ploy to get her own way yet again. She made it look like the warlocks had made the first move and now the fairies would want revenge. Lady Malaga cast out again and made the warlocks mad with fury all except me. Her evil laugh filled the air and she vanished.

I had to come up with a plan quickly, the warlocks all around me were being filled with rage and the fairies would soon be on their way to exact their revenge. The fairies may seem sweet and innocent at first but we all know they had a bad temper. Imagine a fairy battle but a million times worse. 'What are we going to do?' asked Ned.

'There must be something we can do surely,' I asked Ned.

A soft voice whispered in my ear 'Use your magic to trick them Joe, I believe in you and you can do it.'

I began to wonder who had said that when I got my answer 'It's me Joe, your Mum.'

'Mum, how are you even here right now,' I asked.

'You will always be my boy, but you've all grown up, you still have plenty to learn. Please remember I am always with you.'

'I miss you Mum, I want to come home now,' I replied

'You will in time Joe, you have an almighty battle ahead of you. Dad and I are with you all the time.' Mum echoed in my ear.

I began to wonder why I could not see my Mum when my question was answered by her again 'I'm in your heart and mind. Everywhere you go, I go.'

This was the best thing I had heard for a long time and gave me the strength to carry on with my mission. I spoke out to my Mum and asked how she was visiting me as I thought that she could only come through the dream box and letters but she told me that as I got stronger and more in-tuned with my magic, the more things I would be able to achieve. I told my Mum that I thought I had let her and my Dad down. Mum replied 'Joe don't be silly, you have made me and your Dad so proud, your powers are growing day by day. Follow your heart and you will succeed.'

'I don't feel that strong Mum but please know I am trying,' I replied.

'Joe this magic is wearing out, please believe in yourself and you will win, you have the strength and magic.' With this I no longer felt my Mum's presence.

Ned shouted out in my thoughts 'Joe, are you ok?'

I replied 'Yes Ned, my Mum was right, I have the power to do this and with your support we will get this done.'

I walked back towards the angry warlocks and knew what I was going to do. I conjured up ten fairies all made from magic to trick the other warlocks, this would give time until the actual fairies turned up and saved the imprisoned ones. The ten fairies I conjured flew all around the training grounds confusing all of the warlocks. I could not believe that my spell was working. I heard one of the warlocks shout ''come on fairies is this the best you've got.'

All of the other warlocks shouted out in unison 'we're not scared of you, give it your best shot.'

More fairies popped into existence at the slight wave of my ring and they began to float up and down, doing somersaults through the air. I wasn't very happy with this spell and could feel me start to lose control of this magic. I had successfully used the illusion spell and in certain lights the fairies would look see through, I hoped the warlocks would not notice.

I shouted out to Ned that I was about to make the illusion fairies come to life and open their eyes, once I did this they would fly over the other warlocks and turn the tide on this little battle. Ned cheered me on through my thoughts and told me to show them what I was made of. I corrected him and told him that we were a team and always worked together.

I shouted out to my illusion fairies 'Fairy wings awaken.'

Suddenly smoke spun out of my ring and filled the training ground, it flew up into the air and covered the fairies causing their eyes to fling open, they were a bright blue colour with a yellow pupil. If you looked directly at them they would be terrifying.

The fairies sang out 'Who are you and why are you staring at us. We have a watcher girls.'

My face dropped to the floor in shock as the spell I had used to conjure up the fairies did not seem to be working anymore. I should be the one commanding them, they should do my bidding and not act on their own accord.

'Don't think you can control us anymore.' One of the fairies laughed out 'Don't make our fairy wings tickle.'

The fairies flew closer to me and I wanted the floor to swallow me up, what I was witnessing was beyond magic of any making I had ever seen. 'Yes that's right Mister, you better be scared of us.' The fairies sang out.

One of the fairies had started to multiply in size and was almost the size of a tree. I was quite sure the other warlocks were witnessing what I was seeing until one of the other fairies said that she had covered the warlocks in an invisibility spell, so they couldn't see anything that was happening. I begged the fairies not to hurt me and explained to them, that I had created them to wear out the other warlocks. 'We know what you've been up to Joe, we see everything. We are the real fairies and not something of your making.'

''Real fairies? You can't be, I conjured you into existence,' I stuttered.

'Whilst you were busy casting your magic, we gained control over your little creatures and hid them under our invisibility spell. Your magic is not as powerful as you thought Joe.'

'You are very clever and I'm in awe of you all,' I replied.

'Quiet, you will see your warlocks dropping one by one until you give us back the fairies you captured,' the main fairy said.

'It wasn't me, it was Lady Malaga,' I shouted over to her.

'Hmmm that's what you would say, if you are trying to deceive us, we will find out and you will be sorry.'

'No wait, what can I do to prove it to you, I was trying to protect you all,' I replied.

'Protect us, don't make me laugh, you want us dead so you can steal our wands. Mother fairy was right all along about you warlocks, you are all the same. You have the master wand… tell us where it is.'

'Please I can help you,' I pleaded with the fairies.

Within a split second the fairy that was obviously in charge shrank back to her original size and flew back to the other fairies and shouted 'Attack.'

The fairies flew over to the warlocks, wands poised to attack, suddenly the air was filled with the screams of the warlocks shouting 'There's the fairies, come on let us get them.'

I could sense a battle about to happen, the fairies began waving their wands and fireworks filled the sky. Some of the warlock's faces had turned bright red with sheer anger as they began running towards the fairies. This was not in my original plan, the fairies were a lot stronger than I ever gave them credit for. They had wiped out any existence of the spell I had created. What had Lady Malaga done by making sure these fairies found headquarters?

Chapter 16

FIRST BATTLE

One of the other warlocks wanted to show off to all of the others, he cast out towards one of the fairies, a spell shot towards her and the fairy countered it with a wave of her wand. The warlock was lifted off the ground, within seconds his empty uniform dropped to the ground, there was no sign of the warlock. The other warlocks ran away scared from this fairy in complete shock with what had just happened. One of the warlocks just stood there scratching his head in a complete daze, suddenly a burst of colour hit the training grounds and a kaleidoscope of butterflies flew past. The fairy shouted at the retreating warlocks 'you're not so big and clever now are you.'

One of the warlocks turned around and shouted back at the fairy 'you can't just do this and think you can get away with it, you will pay for what you have done.'

'Shut up you stupid little girl.' The fairy shouted whilst waving her wand, the girl's body started to transform and before me stood a pink pig.

All the other warlocks stopped dead on their feet, they dropped to their knees and one of them spoke out 'Please Fairies, don't hurt anymore of my friends, what do you want from us?'

The fairy began to wave her wand and suddenly had a change of heart, the tip of her wand glowed a bright blue and it sounded like a firework had burst into the sky. The fairy turned to the warlock and said 'You have twelve hours to get the master wand back, if you fail your friends that we transformed into a pig and the butterflies will remain that way forever.'

With that, all of the fairies grouped together and pointed their wands towards the ground. They all lit up blue and they shot up into the air quicker than any bolt of lightning. They were gone, I shouted out to the crowd, 'Can't you all realise what Lady Malaga has done, you are all her slaves and she makes you do the most stupidest of things?'

The warlocks agreed with me and they said they could get the wand back. A voice spoke out in the crowd and shouted 'Are you mad, do you really think we can walk up to Lady Malaga and ask for the wand back.'

All the warlocks spun around to see where the voice came from. I noticed a figure walking towards us, it looked familiar but with the fading light, I couldn't work out who it was just yet. As the figure got closer, I finally realised who this was. Blue was walking towards me rolled by hundreds of other warlocks, all wearing uniforms that were blue. I ran over to Blue and pulled him into a hug, tears flowing freely from my eyes. 'Hello my old friend, I can see you've been busy.' Blue spoke.

'Blue, you were trapped....How did you escape from the realm of the mirror?' I asked

'No mirror will ever stop me from fulfilling my destiny Joe, I am rather powerful or did you forget that?' Blue chuckled.

'Where have all these warlocks come from Blue?' I asked.

'Funny you ask Joe, I have been busy myself, this explains why I have taken my time. Where these warlocks have come from is not your concern just yet, all you need to know is that they are your army and have come to stand beside you. Joe I believe you are finally ready,' Blue said.

I shrugged my shoulders and sighed, Blue walked back a little and said Joe, you need to start believing in yourself, you know that I do and how would your Mum have spoken to you if you weren't ready?'

'Yes Blue, I understand, did you see what Lady Malaga did, she turned the fairies against the race of the warlocks?'

'We all knew that would happen, if was only a matter of time, come on Joe, let us finish this once and for all. You have your army and I can feel the power flowing from you. You have everything you need to make this battle go down in history books forever. There have been whispers across the land that Lady Malaga is going to create a dark magic spell this evening and we have to stop her.'

Blue shouted out to the other warlocks and none of them were paying attention, Blue wanted to show me that I am all of their support. Blue cast a spell and within seconds the warlocks were jumping all over the place, Blue turned to me and said 'That's one way to get their attention….Stinging them on the bum!'

Blue shouted out to the other warlocks to pay attention or they would get another sting. He asked them all what he had just asked them to do and they all shouted back that I had and they would stand by my side until the end of this battle. Blue smiled at them all and said 'Remember what I taught you all, you need to be on your guard at all times. Who knows what tricks Lady Malaga will try and pull?'

Blue turned to me and laughed, it was so good to see him and the support that he had rallied felt incredible. It had lifted my mood and I suddenly felt that anything was possible. I waved my ring in the air and felt magic pouring out of me, it covered all of my followers in a purple hue and I knew that they were all protected for what was about to happen. Lady Malaga had better be a little scared, I looked around and noticed that we were the only ones left. Where had everyone gone and why was it so quiet?

Something didn't feel right, there were normally warlocks scattered everywhere, the place was even void of teachers. Joe stopped and called for the warlocks to halt. 'Wait everyone, something doesn't feel right. This smells like it is a trap, we all know what Lady Malaga is like.'

A cackling voice filled the air 'You never fail to amaze me Joe.'

She suddenly appeared floating through the air, her wicked grin etched onto her face. She raised her arms above her head and slammed them back to her sides. Power rattled through everyone's teeth and a loud popping sound caused everyone to cover their ears to protect them from any damage. Suddenly a rustling of leaves attracted our attention, behind Lady Malaga stood hundreds upon hundreds of trees. 'Well it has been nice knowing you all, but as you can see my magic has had a little upgrade. These aren't any trees these are the trees of death.'

Lady Malaga then threw herself higher into the air so she could get a better view of the battle. She then shouted down to us all, 'Let me get myself comfortable, this is going to be a good show.'

Lady Malaga then circled her fingers in front of her and the most beautiful chair you could imagine popped into existence. It reminded me of the furniture from Uncle Barry's house. It was covered in gold leaf with an enormous red velvet cushion. Lady Malaga flew towards her chair and watched who was going to strike first. She started to cackle her evil laugh and pointed her fingers directly at me 'It is not your time to die Joe, watch as your friends fall foul of my trees.'

A green cage appeared next to her chair and I was lifted from the ground and slammed into the cage. She turned to me and said 'You think I'm evil, I promise you haven't seen anything yet.'

I thought about escaping and raised my ring to cast out, power erupted throughout the cage and turned it a bright yellow colour. Lady Malaga had thought of everything and blocked me from using my powers. Ned spoke out in my thoughts 'Joe, they are done for, you did your best.'

I didn't reply, I just sat and watched the stage play out below. Lady Malaga got up off her chair and floated down to the ground. 'This is your last chance, join me and you will be spared from meeting your doom. Become part of my army or die.'

Lady Malaga clicked her fingers and rows of golden chairs appeared. Above them massive lights spelt out Malaga's Army. She floated towards the chairs and said 'Make your choice, you have two minutes as you can see my trees don't like to be kept waiting.'

Several warlocks cast themselves into the chairs and sat down. Once they did the blue uniform vanished and was replaced with a black uniform, the only hint of colour was a golden LM on the left arm. The ones who had chosen the chairs looked happy with themselves as they had chosen to save their own skins. I couldn't be mad at them at all, they were just looking after themselves.

Lady Malaga looked at the other warlocks standing there with Blue. She waved her hands above her head and covered the air in a thick black smoke. I couldn't see anything from within my cage up in the air and dreaded what was about to happen. I heard Lady Malaga shout out 'Now my trees, do your worst.'

A whistling sound hit my ears and I threw my hands to cover my face. I knew what had happened and dreaded finding out for sure. Lady Malaga flew back up towards my cage and said 'I will be back for you, don't you worry about that.' She spun in the air and another cloud of smoke covered her and the golden chairs had disappeared from my view.

The cage that I was in slowly started dropping towards the ground, as I got closer to the ground the black smoke started to thin and I could see my army of warlocks and Blue lying on the ground. The cage sprung open and I quickly jumped out of the cage. I ran towards Blue and the other warlocks and noticed that they had started to fade away. I dashed towards Blue, but the closer I got, the further away he seemed to go. I noticed a bright red door appear in front of me and wondered if this was a parting gift from Lady Malaga or Blue. I hoped it was Blue's last magical creation. I looked down at the door and etched into a golden plaque on the door read 'Back Home.'

I walked around dazed with tears streaming down my face, why had I let this happen to my army and Blue? This wasn't how this was supposed to go. I wrenched open the door and walked through it without a second glance.

Chapter 17

RETURN HOME

The magic that pulled me through the door was unlike anything I had ever felt before. It felt like the magic was expecting me and had missed my presence. The feeling came to an abrupt end and I opened the other side of the door and walked out onto the street that ran up to my house. I ran up the road and saw the house and everything I had missed for such a long time. I walked up to the window and saw Uncle Barry along with my mum who was handing him a cup of tea.

I began to think why Uncle Barry was at ours, he had never visited in all the years we had lived there. I couldn't contain the excitement coursing through my veins. I opened the door and shouted out 'I'm back everyone, did you miss me?'

My Mum ran out of the kitchen and I heard a crash, which I assumed was the cups of freshly brewed tea. Mum reached me and pulled me into the biggest hug I had ever felt. I asked where Dad and the other Joe was and the look on Uncle Barry's face said it all. 'Can someone tell me what has happened?' I shouted out.

Uncle Barry asked my Mum if he should be the one to tell me and my Mum nodded her head sheepishly. I walked into the living room and sat down, Uncle Barry started to brew some tea with his magic. I looked over to the window and thought what would the neighbours think if they looked in the window right now.

Whilst I waiting for the tea to brew, my Mum walked out of the room muttering under her breath. I attempted to listen to her but could not make out what she was saying. Something felt odd and I knew I had to get to the bottom of it. I started to get annoyed with all the cloak and dagger from Mum and Uncle Barry and shouted out at them 'someone just tell me what's happened.'

My shout had startled Uncle Barry that much that he lost control of his spell and the tea cups went smashing to the floor covering the rug, some of the tea even splashed up the walls. Uncle Barry's face was a right picture, I could not stand this a minute longer and cast out at the broken mess and transformed it into a pool of slithering snakes. I knew one bite from my nastiest creation would prove fatal. 'Joe, what are you doing, you are going to hurt someone?' Mum shouted.

She looked at me with horror in her eyes and Uncle Barry scuppered to the corner away from my snakes. 'Tell me right now?' I shouted.

I made the snake hiss at Uncle Barry as it edged closer and closer towards its target. My Mum snapped her fingers and the snakes disappeared and the smashing sound pulled me out of my little trance. The mess that Uncle Barry had caused was back all over the rug. I dropped to my knees and breathed out, this felt like the first breath I had taken for several minutes. Lady Malaga appeared above me and my vision started to weaken. 'What a lovely welcome, you never do learn do you Joe?' Lady Malaga spoke out.

My Mum was angry at the sudden intrusion and shouted to Lady Malaga 'No you listen right now.'

Before she could continue Lady Malaga started to laugh and shouted back 'Now you listen to me.' She threw her hands out in front of my Mum and was lifted off the ground.

'Please stop all this,' Uncle Barry cried.

'You never change do you, you snivelling little man.' Lady Malaga also lifted Uncle Barry off the ground and held him suspended next to my Mum.

'Both of you listen, we had an agreement. You received a letter from me. We agreed that Joe could come home for a little while as long as you gave me his clone. Where is he... hand him over.' Lady Malaga screamed at my Mum.

'You are correct Lady Malaga, we did agree to that, the clone and Jake will be back through that door any minute,' my Mum answered.

'You evil witch.' I heard Uncle Barry shout filled with rage.

'I'll give you evil, how dare you mock an agreement that we had,' Lady Malaga shouted back.

I heard my Mum shout out, 'Please stop it, don't hurt anyone.'

I heard Lady Malaga cackle and said 'I see them walking towards the house, remember our little agreement. You sacrificed one son for the sake of another... and you call me evil.' With that she was gone and left her evil cackling ringing through our ears.

As soon as Lady Malaga had left, Mum and Uncle Barry came floating towards the ground and my vision started to come back. I wondered what had happened and why everyone was staring at me. I couldn't remember a thing. I got up off the floor and wondered what had happened. I turned around to see Uncle Barry and Mum look shell shocked. I said 'Hi Mum, Hi Barry, it's so good to see you.'

The front door opened and my Dad walked in. 'Hi son, it's so good to see you, come and hug your old Dad.'

I ran over and wrapped my arms around my Dad and breathed in his comfortable scent. Once I had hugged my Dad, I stepped back and said 'Where's Joe, my brother, is he in our room?'

I ran to the bottom of the stairs and shouted for Joe to come down and see me. I got no answer and shouted louder that we could play video games later on. I still didn't hear anything and began to wonder where he was. I knew something was up and walked back into the living room and asked what was going on. I noticed a fresh pot of tea and my favourite chocolate chip cookies on the coffee table. Dad was the first to speak and said 'come and sit down son, we have something to tell you.'

I walked up and made sure to grab a handful of cookies on my way. I sat down next to Uncle Barry and he snapped at me 'Enjoying those cookies are you Joe, well make sure you savour every mouthful as that is your last.'

'Barry, that's a little bit harsh.' My Mum shouted back.

'Well he didn't even wait, or he didn't grab a plate... dropping crumbs all over the place like he owns it.'

Uncle Barry obviously forgot that he didn't live here and this wasn't his house. My Dad got into a right rage and bellowed at Uncle Barry 'Keep your opinions to yourself in my house Barry.'

Uncle Barry shrugged his shoulders and said 'Just get on with it will you, I have to get home soon.'

'Joe your brother isn't here' my Mum said quietly.

I asked what she meant and got no answer from my Mum so turned and pleaded to my Dad. Dad replied that Lady Malaga had him now. I screamed out in utter shock and said that he needed to be kept safe and that she should not have him. 'We are sorry Joe, we were desperate to see you and needed to give something in return to be able to see you again. Please forgive us.'

'We have to do something, we can't let that evil witch have him,' I shouted in disbelief.

'I have something to show you Joe, can you please pass me the letter Stella,' Dad said to us both.

I grabbed the letter and ripped the note from within the envelope.

Dear Jake and Stella,

This is our agreement that your son Joe Stone will be allowed to leave my realm and come back for a visit. If you agree then you will swap him for his ghastly clone. If you fail to meet my terms, the clone will forever become one of my army. This agreement or letter cannot be destroyed with magic either of mine or your creation.

You also agree to imprison Joe in a cage for this is the time that the strong will win and the weak will die.

Sign this letter with a drop of blood from you both and this agreement will become magically binding and your precious son can come home for a while, once this letter begins to fade, Joe will return to face me and do what he has been training to do all these years.

Yours Sincerely

Lady Malaga

I dropped the letter in complete shock and raced to my room, I heard my Mum running after me, she followed me into my room. I jumped onto the bed and covered my head with my arms. She spoke softly and said 'It is ok Joe, don't be sad, me and your Dad needed to see you and this was the only way. It is done now.'

'It is done is it, did you know you've sacrificed my best friend Blue and my army of warlocks all so you could see precious little me.'

'It is not like that Joe, it wasn't that easy, you have to believe us,' Mum replied.

'Get out of my room, I wish I had never come back.' I shouted at her.

'Joe please.' Mum said with tears dropping onto her cheeks.'

'Get out NOW! I don't want to hear your pathetic excuses,' I shouted.

I heard my Mum shuffle out of my room and pulled the door shut. I heard her speak through the door and say 'when you're ready, we will tell you everything. I know you need some time but know that we all love you and we would do anything for you.'

I threw my bedside lamp against the door and it created an almighty bang. I heard Uncle Barry shout up the stairs 'Leave him to calm down Stella, he will be down when he is ready.'

I threw myself back on my bed and dozed off to see if this would ease some of the anger that was coursing through my body. After a few hours I woke up and I thought I would show my face downstairs. I walked into the living room and the whole room went silent. 'I will not get over what you've all done, innocent people have died but I'm ready to hear what you all have to say. I haven't got much time as the letter had already begun to fade.'

Mum started to speak out with a wobble in her voice and her hands were shaking. I think she finally realised that I was not her little boy any more and that I had grown up. Dad took over and said 'We get why you're upset Joe, but Lady Malaga threatened everyone we had ever cared about and that was too much of a risk to take.'

I dropped to the floor and covered my head, Mum came over and wrapped her arms around me and said 'It is ok Joe, we totally understand your emotions. We didn't think Lady Malaga would carry on such a heinous act. Don't you worry though Joe, this time she will pay and we will defeat her once and for all.'

From that moment on, I knew I had changed forever.

Chapter 18

THE HEART

In the few hours that I had been asleep the letter had started to fade and by the looks of the letter, I had about three hours left here before my return to the headquarters. There was so much going through my head but I made the conscious decision to not let this disrupt the time I had with my family. We all decided to sit together and come up with a plan that would help me during the onslaught that would be Lady Malaga. My Dad called out to Uncle Barry 'Barry, you should get practising the heart spell.'

'Heart spell.' I gasped

'Yes Joe, it's a spell that if mastered correctly, the spell latches onto the heart that it is cast at. It starts at the feet of the person and will begin to pepper their clothes in red. This could be the best spell that you could take onto the battlefield with you.' Uncle Barry told me.

'Don't put ideas into Joe's head Barry, he has enough to deal with,' my Dad shouted.

I replied to both my Dad and Barry 'If this could work, then I will learn this spell to have in my arsenal.'

'What have you done Barry, if Joe masters this spell, then Lady Malaga will come for us all?' My Dad boomed at Uncle Barry.

I exclaimed 'What do you mean Dad?'

'Don't listen to them Joe, come on catch this,' Uncle Barry said.

He threw a box at me that had seen better days. It looked hundreds of years old and knowing Uncle Barry and his hoarding tendencies, it probably was. I looked inside the box and saw several dried up flies littering the bottom. My Mum chose this moment to speak out 'Oh not this box again Barry, can you not remember what happened last time, do you really want to repeat history?'

I asked out 'What happened last time?'

'You really don't want to know Joe,' My Dad said.

'Joe, just listen to me and ignore those party poopers, what I am about to teach you is very advanced magic. This spell has the power to rid someone's heart of evilness, but of course there always is a price' Uncle Barry said.

'A price…. What do you mean?'

'Well if you master this spell and manage to change Lady Malaga's heart, then a red heart will appear in the box. If this is not done correctly though, the caster pays the ultimate price and the darkness that the box would contain could flow inside the caster, potentially turning them evil forever,' Uncle Barry explained.

'So you're telling me that I could turn evil, if I don't manage to cast this spell correctly.'

'Yes Joe, you're correct but this is our last chance and with desperation comes crazy magic.'

My Mum scolded Uncle Barry and shouted at him 'Barry, this is my son's life you are talking about, what if he changes forever?'

'Mum, if this is really our last chance at defeating her once and for all, then I need to be able to do what I need to do. Barry teach me.'

I picked up the box, and gasped as a sharp shooting pain shot through my hand. I looked down and noticed a few drops of blood had splashed onto the box. I noticed a small stab wound on the palm of my hand. The box started to glow a bright white and jumped from my hands and floated in the air. 'Ouch, you didn't say it would stab me Barry.'

Uncle Barry started to belly laugh at me and I could tell my parents were not impressed in the slightest but there was nothing that they could do. The box opened its lid and I felt a powerful pulling sensation around my chest. If felt like I was being pulled into the box when suddenly the pressure eased. I rubbed my chest and began to wonder what had caused such an odd sensation. I looked over to the box and saw that inside was a heart. Uncle Barry looked over at me and said 'Come on Joe, say the words.'

'What words, I can't see them,' I exclaimed.

'Pay attention and look closer,' Uncle Barry said.

Within a few seconds, a few words started to appear along the edge of the box. They glistened red in the light and I had an eerie feeling that this was my blood creating this magic incantation.

Seek out the heart and make it good, but if you fail we will make good use of your heart in hell.

I spoke out the words and the lid of the box snapped shut and dropped to the floor. The lid was so clear and I could see right through the box and believe it or not, I could see my heart pumping away absent of my body.

'You have done it Joe, you are so powerful, Lady Malaga does not stand a chance against you. When you next meet her, you will notice a slight tinge of red across the bottom of that disgusting dress she wears,' Uncle Barry stated.

Suddenly a huge crash made me jump, the lounge mirror had been forced off the wall and smashed to the ground breaking into hundreds of glistening pieces. The pieces flew through the air, I reacted as quick as I could and cast out a protection spell but I was not fast enough. Uncle Barry dropped to the floor and clutched his stomach. I dashed over to him and forced his hands away so I could get a better look. I gasped when I saw a large splint of glass sticking into him. My parents dashed towards me and pulled me back inside the protection bubble, I looked around our living room as the glass continued bouncing around the room destroying everything in sight. 'Joe there isn't anything you can do now, we warned Barry of the consequences, but he never listens.' Dad said.

'We have to do something, we can't just leave Uncle Barry, he's really hurt,' I shouted at my parents.

After several minutes of the glass pounding the room and ripping everything apart, it suddenly stopped and the glass dropped to the floor. Suddenly Uncle Barry was thrown into the air and screamed out in pain.

'Well, I can see you're up to your old tricks again old man.'

Lady Malaga was standing in the middle of the room with the glass suspending all around her. She lifted herself off the ground and magicked a candle out of thin air, it flickered in the breeze. 'The only light I have is that of this candle. How dare you think you could use this spell against me…. Look at that ghastly red smudge you've given me.'

Lady Malaga pointed at Uncle Barry and he started to float towards her, she swiped her nail across his palm and said 'You wanted me to have good in me, well if your spell works, you will be bound to me for all eternity. I will break your spell and then it will be goodbye to you.'

I shouted out and said 'No, it was my spell not his, you can't do that.'

'Quiet, you dirty little rat. I've had enough of you,' she shouted back at me. She pointed at the wall and I was forced against it, the wall had seemed to gain its own life force and something grabbed both of my hands and legs and pinned me there.

'That's better, now pay attention for once in your lives, there is a battle coming so I have to go and get ready. Joe, I will see you very soon.'

She let out a laugh and swished her hand through the air and healed his stomach and said 'Let this be a warning to you, don't try and take me on, the world will pay for your interference.'

Before I could say anything, she slammed her fist into the wall and it collapsed causing a huge mess. She spun around and disappeared leaving just a faint outline of her dress behind. I dropped from the wall and walked over to Uncle Barry and said 'we can't let this spell continue, it will kill you.'

'It's too late for that Joe, Lady Malaga will continue to get weaker as the spell weaves its way through her. If we stop this spell, it will be you that gets the darkened heart and I will not let that happen,' Uncle Barry explained.

Uncle Barry picked the box off the floor and placed it on the table. 'Lady Malaga will do everything in her power to stop this spell, but nothing can stop it now. It will eventually make its way to her heart.'

'And when it reaches her heart, what will happen?' I asked.

'That all depends on you Joe, the heart in the box will make the ultimate decision. Whoever has the fairest heart will keep their's and the other will be forced to enter another realm,' Uncle Barry said.

'Another realm.... how can this be possible?' I asked

'Let's not worry about that now Joe, your time is nearly up with us.'

I had the feeling Uncle Barry wasn't telling me the truth but I could not question him. I heard Ned's voice inside my head 'Glad you were thinking the same Joe.'

'Ned you are awake, you've been quiet for a long time, I wondered where you had gone,' I said

'Well when you've got feet that smell as bad as yours for company, you're left with no choice but go to sleep. Either that or pass out.' Ned laughed.

'Don't be cheeky Ned, did you notice something odd with Uncle Barry?' I asked

Before I got an answer Uncle Barry raised his hands and the sounds of lightning crackled within our house. Standing right in front of me was my clone but most importantly my brother was back. I shouted out for him to come and give me a hug. He laughed when he saw me and said 'That's right brother, it is me and look how I've played you yet again.'

Joe looked around and noticed that he was no longer in the house but somewhere deep inside a forest. I shouted out at the other Joe and said 'How could you do this after everything I've done for you?'

'Oh stop whining for once, thanks for those drops of blood back there. How could you be so stupid to fall for that old feeble magic?' The other Joe shouted at me.

I began to speak when the other Joe shouted over me 'You always thought you were the best didn't you. Well I made sure you were played good and proper this time. Don't you worry Mum, Dad and Uncle Barry are safe with me.'

'Wait are they not here with us?' I asked

'You Joe, always did fall for everything, it is all just a bunch of spells, come on we have a battle to get to and I want to make sure I get front row seats.' With this the other Joe cast out and we both vanished.

Chapter 19

SECOND BATTLE

I knew that I had arrived at the headquarters with the sounds that filled my ears. Evil laughter was echoing all around. I opened my eyes and the other Joe spoke out 'Lady Malaga, I have brought you Joe back just like I promised, now you must keep your end of the bargain.'

'Bargain, don't make me laugh,' Lady Malaga screamed out.

Lady Malaga was high in the air in her golden chair. She flicked her wrist towards the other Joe and he was pulled right up before her. The other Joe was caught off guard and start to splutter 'What are you doing, I am on your side. I have brought Joe and his family here. Didn't you see my epic smoke screen, I made even you look convincing.'

Lady Malaga started to cackle and said 'You're so weak, you couldn't even make paper float. That awesome show of magic was me. How dare you take credit for something that I am responsible for. I can't even stand looking at you and when I'm finished with you, you'll never see daylight again.'

Lady Malaga grabbed hold of the other Joe and tapped his shoulder, he was thrown backwards into the air and came crashing down to the ground. I was just in time and cast out to save the other Joe from face-planting the ground. Lady Malaga looked over at me in disgust and said 'well after all this unnecessary stress, we may as well get on with it... release the curtains.'

Within seconds the air was filled with floating curtains that twisted and turned, manipulated by dark magic. One of Lady Malaga's warlocks cast out and they burst into flames, I could feel the heat licking at my face. Lady Malaga looked positively gleeful and said 'Oh how lovely...the same colour as my dress Joe, don't think I've forgotten about that.'

I looked around and saw the golden chairs were still there, I made out my Mum, Dad and Uncle Barry's face in the crowds. There were fairies with chains wrapped around their wrists sitting on each of their shoulders. Their wands balanced perfectly pointing towards my family. 'Leave my family alone, you loathsome witch,' I shouted.

'Do you really think that's the correct way to speak to me, you're about to learn things the correct way very quickly. If you fail any of the challenges or battles I set, I will make the fairies pull stones out of your precious loved one's rings,' Lady Malaga shouted at me.

'Wait, you can't do that, you could make them really unwell or kill them. Please don't do that,' I replied.

'Silence, you will do as I say. I need to know who I will be facing when it is time to battle to the death. That will be you who is dead by the way,' she screamed with a pure evil tone to her voice.

Lady Malaga waved her hand in the air and the master wand popped into existence, I began to wonder how she had done this but it was too late, she whipped the wand down towards me and the ground began to shake with the rumblings of thunder and crackling sounds of lightning. I spun around to face my family to check if they were ok, Lady Malaga just laughed yet again. Trees began to pop up all around me and they pointed their branches towards me in a menacing way. I began to cast out destruction spells one after the other. Each of my spells hit trees square on the trunk and each one blew up into millions of pieces. Lady Malaga could see how strong I had become and worry flickered across her face momentarily. She waved the wand sneakily and I dropped to my knees.

One of the trees appeared right next to me, it fired out a branch from its trunk and it smacked into my leg with an amazing amount of force. I couldn't move as the branch had pinned my leg to the ground. I would not give Lady Malaga the satisfaction of knowing that she had hurt me.

I looked up at Lady Malaga and noticed that the red in the dress was nearly touching her heart. It glowed momentarily and Lady Malaga clutched her heart. She looked down at the horror that was on my face and flicked the wand towards me. I was certain this spell was going to be my doom but I was wrong. The branch materialised into nothing and my leg showed no sign of injury. Why had she had the change of heart and was the heart spell really working, was she starting to feel warmth run through her cold dead heart after all? She looked at the tree, and sent a spell careering towards it, the tree moved around just as the spelt sent it smacking backwards into the ground, all that was left were tiny pieces of wood that peppered the ground all around me.

Before anyone could say anything, she again cast the wand towards the sky and disappeared. I looked over to my family and they started to float towards the ground. The fairies that had kept them prisoner flew off away from them free from the chains that had imprisoned them. I heard one of them mutter 'The heart spell is unstoppable, it looks like it could be working, don't tell Lady Malaga though or we would end up as fairy dust.'

Uncle Barry ran over to me and shouted 'Joe did you just realise that Lady Malaga saved you.'

The other Joe piped up and said 'Your spell is working then.'

I heard Ned shout out in my head for the other Joe to keep his mouth shut. I walked over to the other Joe and shouted 'How could you turn your back on your family, what could have made you want to do that? After all the love and support we have always shown you.'

'Please Joe, I was under the influence of Lady Malaga, it wasn't me,' he replied.

'What influence and what spell, you went out of your way to destroy this family, Uncle Barry could have died and if the heart spell hadn't worked, I would have died also? Think about that for a second,' I shouted.

'Joe please, you have to understand, that was never my intention. I'm good, I promise,' he whimpered at me.

'Stop, both of you. We will sort this out later on, I really fancy a cup of tea and some of your Mum's homemade cookies,' Dad said.

'Cookies....Jog on Jake, all I want is my nice cosy bed, all this stress has worn me out,' Mum replied.

My Mum raised her hand in the air and my family were gone in a flash. I raised my hand in the air to cast out but there was an almighty bang as the spell that was about to transport from this place backfired. The spell hit the ground and flashes of light dashed everywhere. I suddenly thought of the bargain that had been struck between Lady Malaga and my parents.

Joe noticed someone running towards him, they shouted out 'Quick you have to hurry, something really bad has happened.'

My heart sank, I was so done with everything that was going on, I thought that Lady Malaga had shown a glimmer of hope a few moments ago but realised that it was going to be short lived. I called out for them to stop and calm down. They told me that Lara had gone crazy throughout headquarters. I told them to stop for a minute and explain properly. They replied 'Lara has turned evil, she has been walking around the headquarters transforming all of the warlock's bedrooms into fear rooms. She has locked lots of people in and not let them escape. One of the rooms has caught fire as the warlock attempted to escape using magic.'

I took off and ran towards the dormitories, as I got closer, I noticed smoke billowing from one of the windows. The smoke manipulated itself into a big ball and Lady Malaga appeared out of nowhere. Her evil cackle filled the air 'How cute are you, running towards your little warlock friends to save them. I've been enjoying my greatest show yet.'

'I knew that it was you, how could you do this to people?' I screamed back at her.

'Well as you know, I'm fantastic at acting. You know that I want you dead, it will make it easier to take what I want from you. The greatest power will be mine. I do enjoy testing you,' she uttered.

I wondered who I was being tested by and then she looked at me and it felt like she was looking into my soul. 'I'm testing you Joe, don't you worry, it won't hurt that much.' Her laughter filled the air again.

'You really are evil to the core, there is no saving you,' I shouted.

'Save me…. You lot took that option away when I was betrayed all those years ago. Some say I hold a grudge, I think of it as comeuppance. You all will pay and suffer in silence.'

I suddenly had a vision flash before my eyes, the box appeared in my vision. I hastily opened the box and looked at the heart inside. The heart was almost all black with very little red left. I knew that my time was running out to save Lady Malaga. I knew the consequences if I failed to save her. My heart ramped up its beating as panic started to flood my body. I could not fail my family and turn into the evil person she had become.

I heard Lady Malaga shout out Lara's name and I was pulled out of my vision. I looked over at Lady Malaga and she smirked and snapped her fingers. Lara appeared in front of me standing next to the dreaded witch. Lady Malaga asked where Lara had been and Lara replied 'Sorry Lady Malaga, I was in the middle of punishing one of those pesky warlocks. I was turning their room into a hot room of water.'

'Well you are almost as wicked as I am, I like it. Remember what I told you about having a great part to play,' Lady Malaga said to Lara.

'Yes Lady Malaga, I am ready to do your bidding,' Lara replied.

'Yes you are my dear, now face your enemies. Joe is one of them them and you need to get rid of him by any means possible.' Lady Malaga cackled and Lara got ready to cast towards me.

Lady Malaga clicked her fingers and time froze, she hovered towards me and whispered into my ear. 'You have no choice Joe, you have to play by my rules.'

'What are you doing, I can't hurt one of my friends,' I said back.

'Joe you will have no choice, I have instructed Lara to rid my headquarters of your presence. She will try everything in her power, the warlocks and precious headquarters will be destroyed by her magic,' Lady Malaga whispered.

'You've planned this all out,' I screamed at her.

'Of course, like I said this will be my greatest show You have a choice Joe, kill Lara and then you can use your little resurrection spell to bring her back. I need to see you cast this spell and then it will be mine once and for all. Once I have your spell, I can bring back the dead and seek my revenge. Your second choice would be to let her destroy everything around us including you.'

I began to think she would stop at nothing to get her hands on my resurrection magic. Lady Malaga walked back towards Lara and unfroze time. Lara shot magic from within her hands aiming directly at me, I dodged out of the way just in time and her spell hit one of the roofs, destroying it into a cloud of smoke. Lady Malaga flicked her wand and the smoke came bellowing towards her and lifted her into the sky. She shouted out over the noise and said 'Kill him.' With this she was gone.

Lara seemed to be in a magical trance and kept firing magic from her hands. I kept shouting over to her to stop but she paid no attention to me. Parts of the headquarters lay in ruins, all caused by Lara's magic. I cast out towards Lara in an attempt to stop her but this seemed to anger her even more. I ran towards the fountain with Lara close behind. I felt the power of a spell blow past my ear and the fountain shattered into pieces, the water shot up into the air, being held there by some invisible force.

I knew that no kind of magic could destroy this water, it will suspend itself in the air until the fountain had been rebuilt. I knew that if I didn't stop Lara, everything would be destroyed. I had to do something, I began to think what I could do when the shouts and screams of the other warlocks filled the air.

Chapter 20

SAVE HEADQUARTERS

The battle between Lara and I kept going on for what felt like eternity. Most parts of the headquarters had been damaged, warlocks were scattered around with scrapes and bruises peppering their skin. I looked over and saw that some of the teachers were sat around the destroyed fountain. They had the ability to siphon the water onto the injured warlocks to help them heal. Another shot of magic tore past me and caused some of the ceiling to collapse in on itself. Was Lara going to keep up this relenting attack or would she see sense? Lara saw what the teachers were up to and went into another crazy rage, the teachers were quick enough to cast out a protection bubble to guard themselves and those they helped from being attacked.

The battle continued and I began to think about the warlocks trapped inside their rooms. What I worried about most was the magic that had been used in this absurd attack on innocent people. When magic was used to hurt then it had nowhere to escape and the magic would continue to build until breaking point. If the magic reached breaking point then all those rooms would begin to implode and severely hurt or even kill those within. Those warlocks were in severe danger. Lara had been totally evil to them and this had been on Lady Malaga's instruction. It was like neither of them cared for anyone anymore even those who had been on their side. She had truly meant it when she said she wanted everyone to suffer.

The word had got back to Lady Malaga about the warlocks trapped and she had sent fairies that had started to do her bidding to keep an eye on things. No one could leave their rooms and I would not be able to get close to help out. I was still dodging attack after attack from Lara, I had no intention of killing her and giving Lady Malaga that satisfaction.

I knew that this would soon have to be a possibility if I wanted this to end, but I knew Lara would have to soon give up with her relenting attacks, she would soon run out of stamina, at least I hoped she would. The ground started to shake beneath my feet and I thought Lara had caused an earthquake with her power consumption but out of the crack, I noticed a friendly face in all this chaos. Silver Lion stuck his head up and said 'Hello, old friend, I can see you are in a pickle but I needed to tell you something.'

'Can you see now is not a good time, I'm rather busy,' I managed to shout out as I dodged a haphazardly thrown fireball.

'Yes I can see that Joe, that's why I am here, let me freeze time for a moment so I can talk to you without you being beaten by a girl,' Silver Lion chuckled.

'Don't start Silver Lion, I don't need your jokes right now,' I replied.

'Joe watch out,' Silver Lion screamed as another fireball came towards me.

I ducked out of the way just in time as the fireball came to a blazing stop right in front of my face. I noticed that the ball of gas was glowing bright red with yellow and orange sparks making up its core. Silver Lion explained that he knew of a way that all this could stop. 'Please tell me, so I don't have to spend anymore time dodging fireballs,' I said.

'Well you know when you cast the heart spell, there is a way to change the course of the spell. If you find a new host for the heart, then you will fulfil your end of the curse,' Silver Lion started to explain.

'What do you mean my end of the curse?' I asked.

'Well if you fail in changing Lady Malaga's heart then you know, you would turn evil, but if you find a new host then you would be free. You can't turn evil Joe, you really can't.'

'Are you saying what I think you are saying?' I asked.

'Yes Joe, you also know I like to keep things safe, so I visited your house and collected the heart as I knew that it would possibly come down to this and I didn't want Lady Malaga's grubby fingers on it.'

I looked down at Silver Lion and noticed that the box had been shrunk with the power of his magic and was balanced between his paws. I gasped as I looked at the heart and noticed that it had nearly changed colour. 'You haven't got much time Joe, your heart spell is coming to an end, please hurry and make your choice. Remember that you haven't completed the spell yet and you are at risk of turning evil. Remember that the new host will also become evil the only solace we would have is that the host would be reborn after one year.'

'A year's time, are you telling me that Lara will be reborn as an evil witch?'

'Yes, but think of it this way, rather than kill her you could weaken Lady Malaga with a new host. This will give you the chance to beat her once and for all.'

I looked over at Lara, frozen in time with a fireball about to be flung my way, her eyes looked kind and innocent but her body language told a totally different story.

Silver Lion spoke out and said 'Make your decision Joe, when you have you need to prick your finger and drop some of your blood onto the heart. Once this is complete make a dash over to Lara and drop some of her blood onto the heart and speak her name.'

I asked what would happen from there and Silver Lion explained that Lara would vanish and return a year later stronger than ever before. I knew that Lady Malaga would be powerful especially with the master fairy wand. Silver Lion carried on explaining that once the transference spell was complete that some of Lady Malaga's powers would be snatched from her to make the new host stronger. 'Quickly Joe, I can't keep time frozen much longer.'

'Ok, I'm ready,' I shouted.

I picked up the needle to prick my finger and dropped some of my blood onto the heart, and said Lara's name. I dashed towards Lara dodging her frenzied attacks, fireball after fireball came close to igniting me on fire. I could feel the heat of her attacks as I got nearer to her. I cast out to freeze her and my spell hit her directly in the chest, stopping her from attacking anymore. I grabbed her finger and jabbed it with the same needle, blood dropped in slow motion towards the heart. As soon as the first drop of blood hit the heart, magic exploded through the air and the heart started to change colour. Another drop of blood hit the heart and the heart began to float its way out of the box and came to a stop in front of Lara's heart. A bright black light flashed through the sky as the heart began to push its way inside Lara's chest, she screamed out in agony, her eyes turned a sinister black colour and there was a crackling sound through the air and Lara vanished. Joe looked around for Silver Lion and he had too disappeared.

Ned shouted out 'What has just happened Joe, something doesn't feel right?'

I was in complete shock with what had happened, I looked back around and saw that the spells that were keeping the warlocks trapped had ceased to exist and the warlocks started to run into the courtyard. Teachers appeared out of nowhere and ran around helping all of the other warlocks. The fountain had been restored to its former glory and looked like nothing had happened or been destroyed in the first place. Thunder rumbled above us and rain started to splash down all around, everyone ran for cover from the rain but the fairies hovered guarding the entrance. One of the fairies shouted out 'No one can enter this place, someone has taken our wands and we want them back.'

The wings of the fairies were ripped from their backs by some unknown force and the fairies dropped to the floor. I wondered what was happening when the same sinister laugh filled the air. One of the fairies pointed towards the sky and shouted 'Look, it's the evil Lady Malaga, and she has our wands.'

The fairies began to run towards Lady Malaga and were lifted up towards her, Lady Malaga's voice boomed out 'My dear little fairy friends, please don't come to my headquarters and start ordering everyone around. You can all get out of here at once.'

Lady Malaga banished the fairies from headquarters threatening them that if they ever returned that she would hunt them all down and snatch the remaining wands. She cast out towards the wands that were floating in the air and they were sucked into the master wand that she held. One by one fireworks were let off from the wand as it gained more and more power.

Lady Malaga shouted out 'All those that are left, you must train day and night to become the best you can be. I will be leaving headquarters for some time, I always have unfinished business. Mrs Evil is now in charge and you will all listen to her. As for you Joe, get yourself ready for our big day, you will hand over what I want or the people you care about will die.'

Lady Malaga struck out the wand again and disappeared. I heard Mrs Evil shout out for the warlocks to assemble to start training and saw that Mrs Green had run towards them to help out. Ned spoke out 'Well it looks like it's just us Joe, what are you going to be training today then?'

'Watch and learn Ned,' I replied.

I cast out and ten trees stood in front of me. Menacing looks all over their trunks, they cracked their branches together in a threatening manner. I ran between them and cast spells from my ring all around me, the trees fell to the ground with a sickening crunch, one of the trees swiped towards my face and I ducked under the attack, I sent a fireball flying towards it and it fell backwards to the ground, defeated. I felt power flow through my body like never before, I turned around to all of the warlocks and teachers, clapping and cheering. The look of happiness all over their faces gave me the confidence that I was strong enough to bring down Lady Malaga.

Mrs Evil walked over to me and said 'Well done Joe, you are truly the one who can stop all of this and save us all. We can't wait to start living our lives the way they were meant to be lived. You'd better get on to saving all those in the gardens who had been turned to stone and all those trapped in Lady Malaga's spell book.'

Ned looked up to me and said 'Yes Joe, I will soon be free and so will my sister. You can do this, I believe in you.'

Mrs Evil thanked me and walked out to resume training with some of the warlocks. I had a little word with myself inside my head and said that I could do this, my loved ones needed me to save them all. I noticed a butterfly flying past me and saw that it was Mr Butter, he shouted 'You've got this Joe.'

Excitement coursed through my veins from all of the cheering and support from everyone around me. I lifted off the ground and a bright yellow glow surrounded the whole of headquarters. I poured as much magic as I could muster into the glow. The people who had been turned to stone started to break free of their stone prisons. I heard Mrs Green shout out 'Yes Joe, you're doing it, you've become so strong and the magic you were born with has made you the best person you can be.'

I looked down at everyone and could see the same hope I could see in the teacher's eyes, that I would be the one to run headquarters. Meanwhile in my head I wondered where Lady Malaga had gone and what she was up to in her leave of absence.

Chapter 21

LADY MALAGA AND UNCLE BARRY

'Pass me that hammer Jake'

'Where is it Barry?'

'Where is it. Are you crazy, the same place it always is on top of the yellow box in the corner.'

I was outside my workshop, working with my brother-in-law and my sister was in the kitchen making her famous cheese scones. I heard my sister shout from the window for me and Jake to play nicely. The smell of those cheese scones made my stomach growl with hunger, we finished what we were doing in the workshop and strolled into my house through the kitchen door. I took my shoes off and noticed that Jake hadn't bothered, I gave him the dirtiest of looks. 'Do you mind taking your shoes off next time, I wouldn't disrespect your house like that?'

I cast out and summoned the mop and bucket cleaning the dirt away that Jake had caused. My sister popped her head around the corner and shouted 'Cheese scones anyone?'

'Yes please,' replied Jake.

'Of course Stella, can you not hear my stomach growling,' I said.

The cheese scones floated from the oven filling the kitchen with the most amazing smells. A plate flew out of my cupboard just in time for the scones to drop on to. They flew over to the table along with a freshly brewed pot of tea and with cups and saucers. I asked where the milk was and Jake shouted 'don't worry I've got it.'

Stella replied 'Wait Jake, I've got everything under control.'

The milk smashed its way out of the fridge and was being pulled in all directions. The milk carton vibrated with all the force that was being applied to it, suddenly it couldn't take it anymore and the carton blew into pieces, splashing milk all over my pristine kitchen.

The anger that I felt was severe, my face felt hot to touch and I could only imagine that it was as red as a tomato. I shouted out to both of them 'Look what you have done to my poor kitchen, not only is there mud everywhere, you've only gone and added milk to the mess. Get out of my sight the pair of you, better still I think you should both leave.'

'It was an accident Barry,' Jake shouted at me and stormed to the kitchen door.

'Come on Stella, let us go,' he shouted.

Suddenly there was a flash of lightning and the wind echoed through my house. It rattled the kitchen so much it exploded sending shards of glass everywhere. Suddenly Lady Malaga stood in the middle of my kitchen, she smirked and said 'Looks like I arrived just in time, you know why I'm here. I'm here for you Barry.'

Lady Malaga flicked her wand around my kitchen and my kitchen table and chairs flew up into the air and were crushed as easily as you would crush paper. The paint from the skirting boards peeled away and started to float through the air, wallpaper shredded before my eyes and the carpet was pulled up and shredded. She shouted out again 'I have always hated this house and your decor, now watch as your house falls to the ground.'

Lady Malaga pointed her wand at the hole that used to be the kitchen window and shouted 'I will have my revenge.'

The wall exploded and turned into dust, I watched as my sister formed a protective bubble over us and Jake pulled her closer to shield her from any evil.

Lady Malaga flew through the now non existent wall and made her way to my outbuilding that housed my workshop. She pointed her wand at my workshop and I saw red, I thought she was about to destroy my life's work. I charged after her and went to cast towards her but I was too slow. She lifted me off the ground and said 'What I want from you is your life Barry, I think you know what I mean don't you?'

She pointed her wand at my chest and unbearable pain coursed its way through my veins, I grabbed hold of my chest as it felt like my heart would burst from within. I heard my sister shout out 'Stop Lady Malaga, you're hurting my brother.'

She cackled her evil laughter and said 'Hurt him, I'll do more than that you imbecile. I want what is mine.'

'What do you mean?' Stella shouted up to me.

I heard Jake echo exactly the same as my sister and Lady Malaga shouted to me 'Go on tell them you pathetic human being.'

The pain left my body and I felt myself fall back to the ground, I felt Lady Malaga's magic still controlling my body. I looked up to her and she laughed again and said 'Well what are you waiting for, tell them?'

She flicked her wand towards me and and I dropped to my knees as the pain flowed through my legs. I screamed out in agony and said 'Please stop, I'll tell them.'

She continued her evil laughter and said 'While you make your feeble announcement, I will make myself comfortable.' She raised her wand and her golden chair materialised out of thin air.

'The reason why Lady Malaga is here, is that she's come to take back her gift that she gave me years ago. I knew this day would come, I'm sorry I haven't said anything but I didn't want to scare you all. When she takes the gift back, then my life will be forfeit.'

'What gift are you on about?' Jake asked.

Lady Malaga looked down at us both, and screamed 'The gift I gave him was my life.'

'I wouldn't call it a gift, I would have called it a curse, she cursed me with eternal life years ago. She handed it over so it couldn't be lost and would be able to take it back whenever she wanted.'

I heard my sister shout at Lady Malaga 'How could you?'

'Stop your moaning Stella, I did this with good intentions. Only I can hold onto this gift. I only gave it away so I wouldn't lose it. This was a gift from my Nan so it is rightfully mine so I can be the only one to live forever.'

I saw my sister's temper flare and she cast a spell towards Lady Malaga in anger. I shouted out for them all to stop this hatred towards each other. I shouted for Lady Malaga to take her gift back once and for all. Stella screamed at me to stop as this would be the biggest mistake I had ever made. 'Enough, I want my gift back and you can watch your brother fade before your eyes,' Lady Malaga shouted.

Lady Malaga flicked her wand towards me and I was lifted into the air, I felt power encase my body and begin to tug at my heart, suddenly my body erupted with a bright glow and laughter filled the air. I looked over and saw the glow arching its way to Lady Malaga and she pulled it into her heart. 'Thank you my old friend for keeping this safe for all this time. I know that it has been difficult living over and over but it's time to say goodbye now.' Lady Malaga said just before disappearing.

I fell to the floor and Stella and Jake ran over to me, they had tears falling from their eyes and grabbed me into a hug. They kept saying thank you time and time again for everything that I had helped them achieve. I pulled out an envelope from my pocket that I always kept there for when this day arrived. I watched my sister rip open the letter.

Dear Stella, Jake and Joe

If you're reading this then my time on this earth has come to an end. Lady Malaga has finally taken her gift back. I want to thank you all for being the best family I could have ever wished for. I know that I can be grumpy at times but please know that I love you all deeply.

Please enjoy my house and workshop as much as I have over the years as this all now belongs to you. Please look after yourselves.

P.S Joe you are going to be the greatest warlock this world has ever seen.

All my love

Barry

I conjured up a chair and slumped into it to spend my final moments vaguely comfortable. I watched Jake and Stella look up and smile at me, they thanked me for the gift of my house and workshop. I watched Jake walk over to the workshop and my sister called out to him 'What are you doing Jake?'

He replied 'Well I am doing what Barry would want us to do, I am going to enjoy this space. Barry must have hidden some rare magical items in here and you know we need to get to our son, he's in grave danger and we need to protect him.'

I watched as my sister walked over to my workshop and jumped out of her skin as my cat sitting guard outside hissed at her. I began to smile when I heard the cat speak out and said 'You lot never learn do you, poking your nose in other people's business. Barry will not be pleased that you are snooping around his workshop. I am warning you that I will claw you if you continue.'

I heard Stella chuckle 'This is what Barry wanted, he will not be with us much longer. Go and say your goodbyes if you want.'

My cat gasped and said 'The gift has been taken off him, how come I was not around when this happened?'

'Wait, you knew about the gift from Lady Malaga,' Stella asked.

'Yes Barry has had me with him for many years. I'm Tim his most loyal friend. Barry saved me from being cold and hungry after I was left tied to a lamp-post by my previous owner,' I heard Tim say as I began to fade faster and faster.

He went on to explain that I had made him a magical cat so that he could live and help others when they needed it most. That cat would have a lot to answer for if I wasn't leaving, spilling my secrets to anyone that he spoke to.

The air glowed around me and I knew that my time was desperately running out, I needed to know that Stella and Jake would find what I needed them to find to help out Joe. Tim turned to Stella one last time and said 'Do me one favour will you, tell Joe not to take Barry's tea next time without asking.'

I heard Jake ask Stella who she was talking to and she explained all about my greatest friend Tim. I heard Stella gasp as she found the mirror that I needed them to find. My mirror was huge and had taken me years to craft, it glowed with the magic that I had imbued it with over the years. I heard Jake say to Stella, 'This is it Stella, are you ready to find our son?'

The next thing I heard was both of them being pulled into the mirror from the little scream Stella let out. I looked down at my legs and thought of the best life I had ever lived, I closed my eyes and the peace and tranquillity took over and I was gone.

Chapter 22

FINDING JOE

The mirror floated to the ground in the middle of the headquarters as Jake and I started to walk out from inside my brother's greatest gift he could have. I missed him more than I let on but I knew I had to save my Joe.

I shouted out 'We made it, where is everyone?'

Jake stepped to my side and said 'Yes we have made it, but where is our son. What has Lady Malaga done with him?'

I noticed a figure running towards me and I blinked away the daze that had settled over me. 'Hey Mum and Dad, what are you doing here?'

I first thought that it was my son Joe, but we had the best ability to tell the difference between a human and someone that had been magicked into existence. This was the cloned Joe and not my son.

Jake called out 'Where is our son?'

'What do you mean Dad? I am your son.'

'We know you're the clone, you had everything from us and you took that all away when you turned evil. We will make sure you pay for what you have done. Remember you are a spell from our making and we can take you away,' I shouted towards the other Joe.

Suddenly a portal opened and pulled the other Joe into it. Then a voice echoed all around us 'You're mine, I want you by my side when the time is right.' A scroll dropped from under the portal and Jake dashed to pick it up.

'Come on Stella, I can hear something and I bet it's the inhabitants of this headquarters. Maybe our son is here after all.'

We both walked over to where the sounds were coming from, it was the screams of the warlocks fighting each other. Spells were flying everywhere in the midst of a battle. A warlock ran towards us and said 'Quick follow me, I will keep you safe.'

'No, I will wait here, I want to see my son,' Jake shouted at the warlock.

'You will follow me, Lady Malaga said you would be on your way. I have a room you can both stay in for the night. We have orders to follow.'

'I heard Jake shout to the warlock 'Are you on her side?'

The warlock turned around quickly and snatched his wand out and pointed it at us both and warned us to follow his rules or we would be dust. We couldn't believe that the warlocks had been given the power to touch fairy wands. The warlock spoke out again and said 'Now follow me, I will take you to your room. We have arranged refreshments for you.'

Lady Malaga had gone all out with this welcome package but I was dying to see Joe, I whispered into Jake's ear 'That evil witch will pay with her life.' The sound boomed all around the headquarters magically.

'It's rude to whisper like that... your whispers will be heard all over our headquarters.' The warlock said.

I took a big breath out and began to wonder if the whole of headquarters were coming after us along with Lady Malaga. We followed the warlock and made it to our room. I couldn't believe what was happening, this was like nothing when I had been a student at this school. The warlock turned before walking away and said 'Get yourself some rest, ready for the big battle tomorrow.'

'Battle with who?' I asked.

He replied 'Why your son and Lady Malaga and only one will win.'

I shouted to Jake to do something and he reassured me that he wouldn't let anything happen to our son. I made him promise and he did with a kiss placed on to the top of my head.

'Well I will leave you both to it, here are your tickets for the best show in town tomorrow.' He dropped them onto the chest of drawers by the door and slammed the door shut. I turned to Jake and said that they were using our son like an old fashioned bull fight and I couldn't bear to watch that. He reassured me again that Joe was the strongest he could be and would survive tomorrow. I kept telling myself time and time again that he would. We both lay down on the bed and Jake pulled me into his arms, I fell asleep after many hours of thinking the worst things I could think of. My eyes finally gave in to their desire to sleep. We both woke up to a booming voice throughout the room. 'Welcome guests of Lady Malaga, we hope you have enjoyed your stay with us, please find all your refreshments topped up, your door will be unlocked ready for the day's show.'

I watched as Jake bolted to the food and salivating to intake as much as he could get this hands on. I looked over and noticed that the food trays were filled to the brim. I walked over and grabbed a slice of pizza, it was odd to be eating pizza for breakfast but I was so hungry I would have eaten anything. A bang on the door made us all jump and a letter was slid under it.

Dear Warlocks and Guests

This letter is in regards to the battle that you will witness today. No other warlock is allowed to intervene at any point. You need to sign your names in blood at the bottom of this letter. Once you have signed you will be bound by magic. Your blood will turn into pink pills that you will need to swallow. Upon taking these pills you will be allowed to leave your room but any use of magic will result in sudden death.

Once the battle has finished you will be allowed to use your magic again.

Lady Malaga

On the chest of drawers a knife appeared. I picked up the knife and made a small cut into my thumb and told Jake to do the same. The instant the blood touched the letter, our signatures appeared and four tablets dropped onto the side. I hastily picked up the tablets knowing that I had no choice but to take them if I wanted to see my son again. I watched as Jake did the same. As we swallowed the door swung open allowing us to roam the headquarters again.

Chapter 23

THE FINAL BATTLE

We went to walk out of the room but were thrown back inside by some unknown force. A warlock peered around the corner and said 'Lady Malaga wants you all to wear what has been provided.'

The warlock waved his wand and a wardrobe began to form in the centre of the room. I went to walk over to it and Jake stepped if front of the wardrobe and told me to wait as this could be a trap. 'Don't be stupid Jake, if it was a trap do you think a silly little warlock could have magicked up its existence.'

'This is Lady Malaga we are talking about,' Jake told me.

I pushed Jake out of the way and pulled the door open, I began to laugh and said 'See I told you that it was ok.'

I began to rifle through the clothes in the wardrobe and held them up to Jake so he could get a better look. I pulled out a long black dress which was covered in gold ropes all laced down the front. Jake spoke and said that I would look like Lady Malaga if I had to wear that.

I began to laugh and held up a black pair of trousers and a long black coat with the same gold detailing on it as the dress. Jake looked disgusted and said that he would not be wearing that. I explained that if we wanted to watch the battle then we had no choice. We both got dressed in silence and hurried through the door. The warlock was holding out a card and I grabbed it, it read,

Welcome to the final battle

Stage One

Both opponents will battle each other but not harm one another in this magical warm up

Stage Two

The opponents will fight each other's armies to the death. Opponents will not be allowed to leave the magical circle.

Stage Three

This will be the final fight and only one opponent will exit the champion. The winner will walk away with the magical stone of the headquarters and become the next leader of this great institution.

Any opponent who breaks the rules will be punished

I looked over at Jake and told him that I hated all of this, he told me not to worry and that our Joe had everything in hand. We made our way to the training grounds and noticed that stands of chairs have been erected and a huge magical circle had been drawn. This was no longer a training ground, it was a battlefield. The hustle and bustle of hundreds of warlocks coming onto the battlefield started to annoy me. Some had even take to making bets on who would win, I was disgusted that people would try and make money on other's misfortune.

I looked around and noticed that every race of magical being had been invited to this place. I noticed ghosts flying over head and fairies fluttering their wings to find the best seats in the house. When Lady Malaga wanted something, she got it and all of these creatures had answered her call. Even the fairies were here, any problems that the creatures had with each other would be forgotten until the battle was over.

We took our seats numbered on the tickets and looked around, some of the warlocks were holding magical candles that were firing sparks of light into the air like fireworks. This was setting the atmosphere and getting everyone but us excited. Suddenly a green cage that had been draped in a black and gold cloak appeared in the middle of the battlefield. The candles that the warlocks were holding started to pour out black smoke and an evil laugh permeated the air. Everyone knew that the evil Lady Malaga was here.

The cage began to smoke and Lady Malaga appeared, she was dressed in her usual long black dress with the golden pattern weaving its way to the floor, the golden ropes started to turn into snakes that started to slither across the battlefield. She took out her wand and said 'Welcome everyone, in the cage in front of you is a warlock who wants to take me on and rule this magical place. I usually welcome anyone who wants to take me on but this is different. He has something I want and rather than take it from him, he will sacrifice his life for it.'

Lady Malaga pointed her wand towards the cage and the magic from the wand hit the cage, the black cloak was whipped into the air and I noticed there stood my son Joe. He looked so different, he wasn't the boy I thought he was but a man who had turned into the most powerful warlock. Lady Malaga shouted across the battlefield 'Ready to face me Joe?' And started to laugh her heinous laugh once again.

I heard my son shout back over her laughter and said 'More than ever, I am more ready than I have ever been.'

Jake and I shouted out in unison 'Come on Son, you've got this.'

Lady Malaga turned her head to face us and shouted silence. The ropes attached to our clothes sprung to life and turned into snakes. I opened my mouth and screamed at Lady Malaga 'I hate snakes you evil little witch.'

Jake turned to me and said 'It's ok Stella, they won't hurt us as long as we do as she says.'

Lady Malaga laughed and said 'My little surprise to you all would be my snakes keeping a close eye on you all. I will warn you all once, a little bite is all that it takes to end any of you. Now let us begin Joe, remember to clear your mind, I won't go easy on you.'

I watched as my son thought he would catch Lady Malaga off guard as soon as the cage was opened. He cast a fireball and sent it streaming towards his target. Lady Malaga was too quick and deflected the fireball, it hit some of the chairs in the crowd causing some of the warlocks to panic. They began to cast out magic without thinking and dropped to the floor, the two tablets working in a sinister way.

'Look what you have caused Joe, people are dying because of your magic, so you like to play with fire do you…I'll show you what real fire looks like,' Lady Malaga shouted.

She flicked her wand towards Joe and a stream of fire erupted from the tip of the wand heading straight towards Joe, he cast out a jet of water which hit the fire and turned it into smoke. Joe waved his hands and the jet of water curved to hit the stands putting out any fires causing the warlocks to panic.

Lady Malaga shouted to Joe 'Sneaky Joe, I will let you get away with that one, no more tricks from you though.'

She slashed the wand through the air again and we all felt the power hit the battlefield. A giant tree the size of three houses materialised out of nowhere. I watched as Joe cast towards the tree and a yellow glow appeared around the base of the trunk, it slowly worked its way through the trunk. I watched as the tree fired branches towards my son and I started to panic, the yellow glow seemed to slow the tree down until it couldn't fire any more branches. Lady Malaga saw that her tree was struggling and in a rage swiped the wand through the air, tiny little stars flew into the sky and latched themselves onto the tree giving it back its strength and eliminating Joe's spell.

I watched Joe cast out again and the glow disappeared, what was he playing at? Lady Malaga gained full control over the tree again. The tree fired multiple branches towards my son and caged him in. The evil witch cracked her wand again and the ground shuddered and knocked Joe off his feet. The tree noticed that Joe was weak and started to march towards him, its branches ripping up the ground as it did.

I knew that my son was in trouble and I almost cast to save him but what use would that have been, if the pills would have killed me. I closed my eyes and buried my head into Jake's arms. I was adamant that I couldn't watch anymore of this battle but curiosity got the best of me. Lady Malaga screamed across the battlefield 'The most powerful warlock, brought to his knees by a simple tree.'

Joe jumped back to his feet and shouted back 'Let me show you what a tree can truly do.'

Joe circled the tree with magic and forced it to turn on its master, it shot out a branch which clipped Lady Malaga's arm, her flesh was ripped open and drops of her blood dripped to the ground. I looked over and saw that Joe was in shock that he had made a tree of Lady Malaga's creation turn on her.

I had met this tree before and realisation hit me like a ton of bricks, I heard Joe speak out 'Sir George is that really you?'

'Yes it's me Joe, sorry about my attack earlier on, I needed to make it look real, I haven't got much time,' Sir George boomed.

He threw Joe a branch and as soon as Joe touched it, it transformed into the most elegant wand I had ever seen. Joe looked amazed at what he held in his hand. Sir George explained that this was part of the wand Lady Malaga had control over and that it was now Joe's. I could have cried in relief to see my son with one of the most powerful magical artefact's in his hand and knew that the tables were about to turn in this battle.

I watched on and before Joe could master the wand, Lady Malaga swiped her wand through the air again and targeted Sir George. I could see the anger written all over her face because a tree had been the one to trick her and not Joe. I watched Joe as he swung the wand through the air for the first time and his magic crackled through the air. His spell also hit Sir George, Sir George's trunk cracked under the sheer pressure of the magic and light from within the trunk flooded the battlefield. Once my eyes had become accustomed to the light, I noticed a man walking out of what was Sir George's trunk. Lady Malaga shouted out 'No, this can't be happening.'

I watched on as Sir George became a man, he walked over to my son and wrapped his arms around him, Lady Malaga watched on with pure shock on her face. Sir George's voice boomed across the battlefield 'Thanks Joe, I will take it from here, he clicked his fingers and the wand flew out of my son's hand and into Sir George's. He pointed the wand at Lady Malaga and a shot of magic was sent straight at her.

Sir George and Lady Malaga continued to battle, the battlefield filled with the flash and bang of spells. Lady Malaga flew into the air to get a better aim at Joe and Sir George. I looked on in amazement as the battle continued to play out. I heard Sir George shout out towards Lady Malaga 'Are you going to tell them or shall I.'

'You won't win George, I will be back and have my revenge,' Lady Malaga screamed.

Lady Malaga whipped her wand through the air and disappeared. We all felt the magic that had been cast over dissipate, we were no longer bound by the magic of the pills. Our clothes began to morph into a new colour. I looked down at mine and Jake's clothes and noticed that they were all yellow now.

I heard Joe ask Sir George what was going on as we hurried over to him. I wrapped my arms around my son and kissed him all over, relieved that he was finally safe. Sir George spoke across the whole of the battlefield. 'You all need to know something, Lady Malaga came to this place and took over, she transformed me into a tree. I am sorry that I have left you struggling for years under her rule. She has gone for now but mark my words she will be back.'

Joe looked at Sir George and said 'What happens now then?'

'Well there is something I have to do, all those that have been changed into something they are not, we need to change back.'

We all looked down and saw Ned begin to laugh on Joe's feet. 'You can change me first, I've had enough of Joe's smelly feet.'

Sir George burst out laughing and pointed his wand to my son's feet, a loud crack erupted around us and a blast of magic flooded the ground we walked upon. Joe's boots disappeared and in their place were a normal pair of boots. Someone tapped me on the should and I spun around and saw Ned laughing at my son. 'Thank you, its been a very long time.' Ned said.

Joe saw that Ned was finally human, he hugged him and said 'Thanks Ned for everything you have done for me on our adventures.'

Ned replied 'No problem Joe, we shall always be friends, come on, let us go and save my sister.'

We walked back to Joe and we both hugged him, 'Well done Son, you've made us both so incredibly proud. We have had enough for now and are heading home, please don't be angry. We have plenty of days ahead of us but for now your Mum and I need to rest.'

We looked around at the sudden applause that echoed around the battlefield, all manner of magical creatures had come to cheer Joe and Sir George. 'Come on everyone, we have so much to sort out, I hear a new witch will soon try to lay claim to this land. We all know a battle is coming between Lady Malaga and Lara.'

Jake and I started to walk back towards the mirror, Joe and Sir George had so much to do and we would let them get on with it. Joe waved us off and turned to Sir George and said 'George we need to make amends with the fairies.'

I chuckled as we kept on walking, there was a bright flash and a pesky little fairy we knew as Flora flew down towards Joe and said 'Hi Joe, I've missed you so much. We do need to make up with the fairies, but don't worry, I have passed on a message to them all saying this was Lady Malaga's doing. They will be here soon and will want to talk to you. Come on my dearest old friend, let us go and save the world from evil.'

Joe

Page 275

Created by Sheralyne (My Mum) Thank you for your amazing artwork and portrayal of Ned.

Left intentionally blank for your imagination to run wild and for you to create your own artwork of the characters from the book.

Left intentionally blank for your imagination to run wild and for you to create your own artwork of the characters from the book.

Printed in Great Britain
by Amazon